Strange Things Happen At

It is this hour when fear

echoes feebly throughout the shadows of the night

and death recognizes no boundaries.

Strange Things Happen At

Murder, Suspense, and
Short Weird Tales by

JACALYN EYVONNE

ISBN 978-1-7354936-2-6 (Paperback Edition)
ISBN 978-1-7354936-0-2 (Hardcover Edition)

Strange Things Happen At MIDNIGHT is a work of fiction. The characters and events portrayed in this book are fictitious. Any similarity to real persons, living or dead, is coincidental and not intended by the author.

Cover Design by Petergraphics
Back Cover Photo by the Author

First Printing October 2020
For information, contact:
author.jacalyneyvonne@gmail.com

Acknowledging my grown-up children who, over the many

years, have allowed me to bounce my stories

and ideas off of them.

My daughter Nicole hates anything horror and will not

watch a scary movie with me, yet took the time to read every

story I have written even though they might

cause her a restless night of sleep.

And, to my son Neuman, the complete opposite of his sister,

eagerly delved into the story concepts with me,

sparking the most ghoulishly fun scenarios.

CONTENTS

1

VENGEANCE

Success came easy for David Michael. He expected to be wealthy at an early age, believing it was in his DNA to become so. He was a brilliant but arrogant young man, an Ivy League school graduate who majored in Software Engineering and Computer Science. He was well vested in the stock market, becoming a millionaire several times over by age twenty-six.

David had always been the popular one, both in high school and college, because of his strong personality and good looks. He was also emotionally manipulating. David knew what he wanted and made sure no one got in his way. He spent most of his days working from home, managing his stocks, and developing new gaming and software apps. Still single, David dated a lot, going from one woman to another, because he could. He was remarkably tall with a masculine, athletic build with stylishly messy brown hair and deceptively sweet brown eyes. A gift from his mother, the sweet brown eyes.

His home was impeccably neat and well-organized. He was quite anal.

The outdoor yard lights barely illuminated across the well-groomed grounds as he looked beyond the kitchen window. His reflection softy peered back at him from the windowpane. An open bottle of champagne waited for him on the counter.

A female voice rings out in the background, "David, hey baby, what's taking so long?"

The ladies loved David. They loved his money, so most would do anything to be around him.

"I'll be there in a minute Jessica," he called back in an impatient tone.

David could not understand why anyone would marry when women lined up to be with wealthy men, plus he did not want to share his money. He earned it; it was all his.

He popped the cork on the champagne bottle, grasped up two nearby tulip shaped flutes, and headed out the room.

The following evening, David relaxed with a glass of wine in front of a large circular fireplace in a room encased in floor-to-ceiling elegant panoramic windows. His eyes closed as classical music gently flowed throughout the spacious single-story home. David sat forward and reached for the bottle of wine. As he refilled his glass, he thought he glimpsed movement beyond the windowpane to his left. Turning quickly, David stared at the window for a moment before returning to pouring his glass of wine.

Two hours passed, the bottle now empty. David grasped the depleted bottle and flute and headed towards the kitchen.

David stopped suddenly, startled by what appeared to be two small yellowish eyes staring at him from beyond the large glass pane. Briefly frozen, he stared, focusing on the eyes.

"What the hell?" David said as the sound of a hiss can be heard from behind the glass pane. Taking a step closer, he could make out the silhouette of an emerald black cat against the darkened night backdrop.

"Fucking cat!" he yelled, sitting the flute and bottle on a nearby console table. He picked up a small paperback book and thrust it against the window. The sudden impact caused the cat to dart away.

David's home sat on three acres. There were no nearby neighbors. He wondered how the cat ended up at his property.

"Fucking cat!" David winced.

David hated cats. He recalled being severely scratched by a cat as a kid. The faint scar from that experience still visible on his right arm. David despised cats to this day. He pretended he was not freaked out by the initial sight of the cat's eyes peering through the windowpane, his heart still pounding. But he was.

Angelina laid scantily clad beside David, both sprawled on a blanket in front of the fireplace. The sweat still glistened across her body from their lovemaking moments before. She was a sleek, beautiful young woman. As David raised to kiss her, he caught sight of the cat's eyes glaring at him.

"Oh, hell, no," he shouted as he leaped up.

Angelina, startled, turned her attention to his actions.

The cat's eyes widened; the hair stood straight up on its tail as it released a guttural groan. David raced over to the window; the cat dashed away before he reached the sliding glass door.

"What is it? What are you doing?" said Angelina startled.

"A damn cat!"

"What?" Angelina chuckled, perplexed by his actions.

"A damn cat! Didn't you see it?"

"A cat? David, what's going on?"

"I hate fucking cats!"

"Maybe it's hungry."

"I'm not feeding that damn cat. I don't want it coming around here. You start feeding the damn things, and they never leave."

"It's just a cat David, what the hell?"

"I said, I hate cats!" His temper erupting.

"David, you're behaving like a child."

"Don't tell me how to behave!"

"Geez, David."

"Get out!"

"What?" Angelina looked quizzically at him.

"Get the hell out!"

"Well, fuck you then!" Angelina snapped back as she raised herself and grabbed her clothing. She headed to the bathroom to dress before leaving.

David peered out across the darkness of the night with a sense of trepidation.

"What the hell do you want?" He muttered quietly to himself.

David spent the day debugging his new gaming app. Many of the games he developed were violent across various genres; his favorites—action, adventure, and horror. He grew up on these games and enjoyed creating nail-biting grisly scenes. His current game app included blood, gore, finite weapons from the first-person shooter standpoint. He immersed himself daily, spending hours testing out his platforms.

It had been a long, tedious day. He stood to stretch from the hours of sitting as he looked across the reddish hues splashing the violet-blue sky. The streams of color spilled across his tree-lined landscape like an enchanting painting.

After a light meal, David scraped the remaining scraps on his plate into the trash. Pulling the bag from the bin, he tied the top and unlatched the patio door. Hesitating, David stared out along the base of the panoramic windows within his sight. He continued to stare before sliding open the patio door and hurrying over to the trash bin. After tossing the bag, he re-entered his home.

A stillness cloaked the house. It was nearing midnight when David woke from his sleep. The classical music that he fell asleep to had stopped.

The floor creaked beneath his bed. David sat straight up, clicking on the nightstand light. He looked around the room… listening. The floor creaked to his left. He jumped out of bed; his bare feet hit the floor as he glanced over his surroundings. Stooping down onto his knees, he pressed his body to the floor and stared under the bed. David's chest was exposed, having slept only in his boxer shorts. As he glanced under the bed, he caught a glimpse of a shadow moving swiftly close to the floor past the open door.

A panicked jolt pushed across his heart. Jumping up, he ran to the doorway and looked up and down each direction of the hallway. Suddenly, the lights went out. The house plunged into darkness. David froze, squinting his eyes into the dark. He clicked the light switch up and down, but nothing happened.

David rushed into the living room. Glimmers of moonlight faintly seeped through the many windows. Staring over the area, he caught sight of a menacing silhouette near the kitchen doorway. Grimacing yellow eyes stared sternly at him.

"No, no, no!" he said, running swiftly towards the silhouette's direction. As he entered the kitchen, his foot slid after hitting a wet spot on the floor. His body hit the floor with a hard thud, and he lay sprawled inside the kitchen door. His back was wet; the smell of cat urine filled the air. Sweat slithered down his brow, his jaw tightened. He pulled himself to a sitting position.

"What the fuck!"

His hip was bruised and painful. His entire back and

boxers were completely covered in cat urine.

David glanced back into the living room. The emerald silhouette stared at him from across the room. The cat's lips appeared to curl beneath squinting eyes before running off into the home's darkness.

David pulled himself off the floor and moved with a slight limp over to the kitchen counter. He gripped the larger knife from the glass block cutlery set and headed into the other room.

He could still smell the cat's urine on his back growing angrier by the minute. There was a deep sense of foreboding within him. The floor creaked in the hallway, and he rushed towards the direction of the sound. Stopping suddenly in his study, he stood silent in the darkness, listening.

A loud hiss overhead, the cat lunged at him from atop the bookshelf against the wall. David dropped the knife as the cat dug its claws into his back. He screamed while grabbing it and ripping the cat from his back. Startled at its touch, the cat slipped out of his grip and ran across the room. Fear covered David's face; the cat's body was icy cold and wet to the touch. He tried to reason with himself, believing there must be an explanation for the frigidity of its wet, cold body. An ear-splitting hiss echoed from the other side of the room, and the cat's eyes glowed frighteningly at David. He grabbed the knife off the floor but was engulfed by a sickening panic, recalling the time he believed he saw those eyes in the past.

David was always unsympathetic and cruel. At times even

brutal. He grew up in rural Minnesota with his parents in an inconspicuous, two-story wooden cottage near a dense, overgrown waterfront.

David spent most of his days in his room on the computer, though his parents frequently insisted that he spend time outdoors on the lake. When he was eighteen years old, he had a run-in with a feral cat the summer after graduating high school.

As David walked through the high bush towards the lake, a ginger-colored wild cat jumped out at him and clawed his right arm. Blood trickled from the wound as he ran back to the house where his mother cleaned and wrapped it up. There was concern in his mother's worried eyes as she sensed how furious David was about his injury.

The following day David took a canvas drawstring duffle bag and his .22 caliber pellet gun into the dense brush, quietly searching for the cat. He found it sleeping and crept into position, took aim, and shot it, the first shot hitting it in the eye. He shot several more times, killing it.

David was proud of his kill. When he approached the cat, he heard faint meows in the background. He shuffled the brush aside and found a litter of six 3-week old kittens. All were ginger except for one, a solid black tabby.

David put the dead feral into the duffle bag, then picked up each kitten one by one and placed them in the bag. As he picked up the tiny black feral, it meowed gently at his touch, locking eyes with him. David put it into the bag with the others, knotted the drawstring tightly, and tossed the bag into the lake.

The bag was found the following day about a mile down the lake. Once opened, all the kittens were dead except for the one emerald black tabby. It was a miracle that it was still breathing. That little black kitten used up every one of its nine lives to remain alive. Word spread throughout the neighborhood about the little miracle kitten and her desire to live. Someone said it was so strong that *It was as though the spirit of Bastet, the ferocious ancient Egyptian cat goddess, entered its body and saved her soul.*

The neighbors all took care of the little kitten until she was older. She was a free spirit and never settled at one home; she spent time with several families. Then one day, the tabby just up and disappeared. The neighbors never saw their shared furry friend again.

David frantically raced around the house, looking for the cat. As silhouetted shadows swiftly brushed past him, he swung the knife feverishly in front of him. With each miss, the cat clawed him, lacerating each eye as David's horrific screams permeated throughout the home. With each blind swing, the cat became more aggressive in his attacks. David grew more tired as the hours passed, and the gashes to his body weakened him as his wounds bled out. When he dropped to the floor out of exhaustion, he dropped the knife. The cat pounced on him and tore into his neck. David let out a gut-wrenching moan as the tabby stood on his chest and looked him directly in his blood-filled eyes.

David remembered.

He convulsed and gasped for the last time as his soul

withdrew from his body.

A week passed before David's body was discovered. Blooded paw prints were found in several rooms of the house, across the floor, and on the walls and ceiling. Claw marks ripped across his torso. His neck was split open, and both eyes were gone. There was no sign of the cat.

2

THE WHARF

Detective Lorraine Russell leaned over a body found beside the dumpster behind a restaurant on Bay Street. A white male brutally slashed to death. His throat was slit, and his body mangled from the violent slashes. He lay in a pool of darkened, nearly dried blood, which also spilled from the edges of his mouth.

"How long has he been here?" she asked the coroner.

"I'd estimate since midnight, at least. I will be able to give you a definitive answer once we can get the body on the slab and cut it open."

"Whoever did this has made your job a little easier; he's cut open pretty good already."

It was nearing 7:00 a.m. The morning was frigid cold from the wind blowing from across the bay.

"Gosh, I wish folks would go home when everything shuts down. This place closes at 10:00 p.m.," said Russell.

Detective Russell turned to an officer on the scene.

"Have you contacted the lounge owner?"

"Yup, they closed at 10:00 p.m., alright. The owner said all the employees were out of here before midnight. They didn't see or hear anything suspicious," he replied.

"Make sure you check with the adjoining businesses."

"Already on it, Detective."

"What about cameras?"

"None back here," replied the Officer.

Turning her attention back to the coroner, "Do we know who he is?"

"Leonard Barrett. He appears to be a tourist from Seattle. He has a hotel key from The Wharf Inn. His ID was in his wallet but no cash."

"Credit cards?"

"Gone too."

"Looks like the same MO as the other four victims," said Detective Russell.

"I would say so, and our perp is making sure he leaves no witnesses behind."

The Officer chimed in with a question. "Do you think he is getting excitement or arousal out of killing?"

"Yeah, well, he's definitely a sick SOB. I'll check the hotel out," she said. "Check in with me when you get your final report together. Push it for me."

"Will do," said the coroner.

Detective Russell picked up her morning cup of coffee from her favorite java house, the Coffee Corner. She was an attractive woman with sandy blond hair who purposely toned down her beauty on the job. Her hair was always pulled back into a shoulder-length ponytail. She wore no makeup except for a natural colored lip gloss. A white blouse peeked through a long sleeve stretch jacket that complimented her narrow leg jeans and flat cushioned walking shoes. Now going on nine years as a detective, Russell was committed to her work.

She always purchased a 2nd cup of coffee for Joe. Joe was a panhandler that sat against the building wall between the coffee shop and adjoining souvenir shop. Joe worked with Detective Russell over the years as one of her informal informants.

The street was already scrambling by 9:00 a.m. with shop vendors setting out sidewalk displays, employees rushing to clock in, and early morning tourists. Joe wore slightly wrinkled clothes, but not dirty like many of the homeless in Haight-Ashbury or the Mission District. Joe was able to sleep on a cot in the rear storage room behind the gift shop. There he could hand wash his clothes in an old but functioning utility sink. Joe entertained the tourists with a tarnished harmonica that garnered enough money for daily meals. He was a skillful musician, becoming a part of the tourist attraction, so the beat cops left him alone.

Detective Russell worked the greater North Beach area of San Francisco, including Fisherman's Wharf, The Embarcadero, the Financial District, and nearby localities.

The Wharf was always bustling with tourists roaming in and out of the restaurants and tacky souvenir shops. She handed Joe his coffee. Joe thanked Detective Russell.

"Keep an eye out for me, Joe. You know you've become my eyes and ears," said Russell as she turned toward her car parked in the red zone in front of the coffee shop. Joe knew about the recent murders. Everyone in the city did; it was big news in the media. He kept his ears to the streets listening for any talk that might help her out.

"You got it," responded Joe as she started up the vehicle and slowly moved down the street.

There were more homeless on the streets than had been in the past. Over the prior few months, the location had become a high-risk area for both tourists and employees.

The visit to the Wharf Inn did not provide much information, leaving the Detective a little frustrated as she entered the precinct. Most of the investigative work on the recent murders had been input into computer platforms that electronically mimicked crime boards. Detective Russell kept a victim binder in her desk with photos and linked information. It was easier to pull out her binder and review notes instead of pulling up information on the computer. She usually left that task to her investigative assistants, which included printing out hard copies from the computer for her notebook.

Her binder had grown thicker over the past few months. When she became a detective, there were very few murders in the Wharf. Back then, she worked assignments throughout a greater area of San Francisco. However, over the past year, robberies and murders increased.

The front section of her binder contained the five most recent killings. However, towards the back were at least eight other victims with the same MO and included photos of each crime scene. Each victim slashed, with the violent cuttings growing progressively worst with each new case. Leonard Barrett was the worse yet. Detective Russell was concerned that the next would be even worse. All the victims were men, most of whom were tourists, except for two locals.

While the cities real estate continued to rise in the new high-tech digital era, there was still the underbelly of violent crime. The robberies had the team looking into gang members that may be infringing into the North Bay during the late hours. Yet, even with nightly patrolling, no clues were leading towards a culprit.

Four days later, a drunk Lucas Harvey wavered down the sidewalk near midnight. The fresh sea breeze from the waterfront chilled the air. He was alone on the quiet, dark street except for an occasional passing car. Harvey was unaware of the shadowy figure veiled in black in the distance, barely visible as he moved past the storefronts. The more Harvey stumbled in his drunken stupor, the shadowed figure inched closer to him.

It was 4:00 a.m. Detective Russell was in a deep sleep when her phone rang.

"I'm on my way."

The crime scene was gruesome. Lucas Harvey's body lay sliced up on the ground beside his car in a secluded parking lot off Beach Street. Detective Russell felt sick; her voice was unsteady as she inspected the body.

"My God, gangs normally use guns; they don't stop and cut up people like this." A look of pure disgust clouded her face.

"Could be some kind of new initiation," commented the lead examiner.

"I... I don't know. Twice in four days. His body has double the number of slashes as the last victim. It takes time to stab someone this many times. Could it be more than one perp?" she asked.

"The stabbing patterns appear to be the work of one person," replied the coroner.

Six hours later, Detective Russell handed Joe his cup of coffee.

"Detective, the word on the street is a homeless guy who hangs out over in the financial district has been showing up with a lot of cash."

"Any description or name?"

"All I know is they call him Soup because he's always at the soup kitchens."

"Soup, huh."

"But I heard he hasn't been at the kitchens as much over the last month. It's like he hit the jackpot or something."

"Anything else?"

"No... except he has long, dirty blond dreads."

"God damn it," she said suddenly as a seagull's poop landed on her sleeve, just missing her coffee cup.

"People say a bird pooping on you is good luck," said Joe.

"Yeah, well, I wish that were true. Outside of the crime, this is the only other thing I hate about this area, too many damn seagulls!"

Detective Russell spread the poop further into her sleeve as she clumsily tried to wipe at it. Joe smiled.

Detective Russell assigned her investigative assistants to do the research. Mark Garcia, her lead assistant, was eager to jump on the case. Detective Russell knew Mark had an appetite for her job and, at times, appeared quite thirsty. It took little time for Mark to identify the description of a slim white man, about 32, approximately 6 feet tall, that also had blond dreads. That afternoon, Detective Russell, along with several patrol cars, flooded the financial district, homeless encampments, shelters, and soup kitchens looking for the person fitting that description.

"Detective Russell!" A male voice blasts from the shoulder microphone attached to her bullet-proof vest. "We spotted the suspect. He took off from outside of a clinic, headed north on Francisco Street!"

"I'm on my way!"

"Shots fired! Shots fired!" The voice shouted.

"Who's shooting? I need him alive!"

Kearny Street was lined with bright flashing lights and

spotlights atop police cruisers and unmarked vehicles. The adjoining streets were blocked off as crowds gathered behind the yellow caution tape. Forensics had arrived. Detective Russell was annoyed as she squatted down beside the victim, surveying the body.

"God damn it! What do you have for me?" Russell asked the senior crime scene technician.

"Shot twice in the torso. We found cocaine in a back pocket, about a hundred ten dollars in cash, and an expired state ID card. His legal name is Brook Swenson."

"His street name is Soup. God damn it!" she remarked in frustration.

"It looks like he was selling the cocaine. He had enough on him to make me believe he was dealing. Likely why he ran," said the technician.

"Who the hell shot him?"

"That young rookie over there, the one standing with Chief Miller," the coroner replied. "I thought he was going to barf all over the Chief for a moment." He chuckled.

At the precinct, Detective Russell was closing in on the last hours of a long day. Her binder spread open on her desk as she studied several of the grisly photos cluttered in front of her.

"This makes no sense... he's dealing drugs. So why is he killing strangers?"

"You don't think this is our Wharf killer?" asked Mark, the lead investigative assistant.

"Whoever did this had to be strong, had to have upper

body strength, to stab someone multiple times like this," she responded. "Soup was skinny. He looked like he used as much of the cocaine as he sold."

"The drugs can make you think you're superman," replied Mark Garcia.

"Yeah, maybe, but something is not adding up," said Detective Russell.

"One of those intuitions again, Detective?" Mark said, chuckling.

"Laugh if you want, but sometimes you need to listen to your gut when you get little feelings about things." Russell shrugged, continuing under her breath, "and I'm feeling something."

"My gut is telling me I need to eat something," Mark replied with a louder chuckle.

"If he was making his money selling drugs, why rob and kill people? Why would the word on the street pin him to these murders?" she quietly asked herself.

Shadows from the trash bins stretched along the narrow driveway running behind the endless stretch of souvenir shops on either side of the Coffee Corner. Detective Russell waited quietly in the dark; her eyes fixed on the storage door to the rear gift shop adjoining the Coffee Corner.

It was near midnight when the door opened to Joe, exiting into the alleyway, cloaked in all black. She sat in the stillness of the dark behind a dumpster and boxes, shielding herself. Once Joe was out of sight, she quickly used a credit card to pop open the storeroom door, pulling out a small flashlight as she entered. A narrow stream of light moved across the small room as she hurriedly searched her surroundings. Glancing beneath the cot, she pointed the beam towards the wall, to a small cardboard box. Russell moved the small bed and retrieved the box. Her heart pounded as she shuffled through credit cards and cash. They were all there, Luke Harvey, Leonard Barrett, and several others.

"You shouldn't be here," Joe said from behind her. Startled, Detective Russell turned, dropped the box spilling the cards and money across the floor.

"I like you, Detective, but you shouldn't be here," his eyes locked on hers.

Joe maintained a quiet distance from the people around him. Listening more than he spoke, Joe, trusted by the homeless community, frequently sharing his food or drink with those in need. Detective Russell was one of the only people Joe enjoyed talking to, regularly feeding her information picked up on the streets. She was kind to him over the years, and he grew to like her.

He appreciated the passerby's that showed him respect. Joe played his harmonica and offered a quiet thank you or nod to those tossing coins into his plastic cup. However, there were many that Joe did not like, many that he regarded with dismay. Those that were rude, disrespectful, and looked upon him with disdain. Losing his house and becoming homeless changed him. It angered him that people no longer saw him as human and disregarded him. He wanted to make them see him; to respect him. He needed to make them pay.

Over the years, his anger grew, his lack of patience increased, and he began to follow those he scorned to their hotels or workplaces. He bounced between trying to control his anger and the desire for revenge. Revenge took control and won.

"Look, Joe, you're a good man. I've known you for years. Let me help you with this! I can help you!" Russell said, thinking she might reason with him.

"I can't let you leave here. I'm sorry, Detective."

"But why, Joe? Why point me to Soup?"

"Innocent people get accused of crimes every day. Soup wasn't so innocent selling drugs to other homeless people." Joe looked fixedly into Russell's eyes. "I like you, Detective. I didn't want it to come to this."

Detective Russell did not turn her attention from his eyes either, preparing for his next move. His eyes narrowed to a penetrating stare. Russell quickly went for her gun. As she did, Joe slashed her right hand, causing her to drop her weapon.

She let out a loud wail as blood gushed out of her half-severed hand. Joe swung his large knife again, lacerating her face. Her eyes blurred momentarily from the spray of blood spouting from the wound. He rushed her; one hand tightened around her throat, the other raised the large knife above him as he hunched over her pressing her body against the wall. Detective Russell quickly kneed him in the groin, causing him to arch over. She dropped to the floor, grabbed her weapon, rolled over, and emptied every bullet into his body.

Sobbing, Russell grabbed the now bloodied sheet on the cot and wrapped it around her half-detached hand. She struggled to release the radio from her vest. Blood continued to spill from her face. Scared and weakened, her voice cracked as she spoke.

"This is Detective Lorraine Russell. Shots fired. Officer needs assistance. Send backup. Rear roadway 292 Fisherman's Wharf."

3

GROVE STREET

The sky was grey as the first glimmer of morning light layered itself over Grove Street. The sidewalks were all lined with bright green artificial turfs and picket fences. The flowers appeared fragrant and readying for full bloom. It was that moment between night and day when the street was still and quiet, except for the sound of the birds beginning to fill the air. One by one, the lights in the windows on both sides of the street began to come alive. Everything about Grove Street appeared to be perfect.

Maximillian, a silky, long-haired white Persian cat, sat on the windowsill of old Mrs. Nealy's house. Widowed for three years, Maximillian had become her closest companion, and the windowsill had become his favorite spot in the house. As Maximillian looked out over the neighborhood, he caught sight of a bird soaring overhead. His eyes eagerly followed its flight as it landed in the weeping willow tree standing in the front yard. Maximillian lowered his head in the direction of the bird and pawed at the glass windowpane between them.

"Good morning, Maximillian," said Mrs. Nealy, lifting him to her chest as she gently stroked the cat's brow. Maximillian still focused on the bird in the front yard.

"Not much to look at these days," she said sadly, glancing out across the lawn. The grass was a striking green right up to the base of the willow tree. Her once prize-winning roses stood nearby along the driveway. Mrs. Nealy could remember a time when the neighborhood was full of life. When she and her husband strolled the block together, chatting with the neighbors along the way. A time when children bounded in carefree play. A time when she could tend to her garden.

"Those were the good old days," she said. "Everything is different now."

Not because her husband Harold was no longer with her after passing away a few years ago. They had a good life together, a full life. She had no regrets. Of course, she still missed him. But, after his passing, she found joy in the friends and neighbors around her. Plus, there was Maximillian, always there to comfort her.

No, the changes were more recent. The children never laughed anymore. There was no more ambling slowly along the sidewalk or enjoying the rocker on her front porch.

There was instead a deathlike stillness haunting Grove Street, an awful, frightening feeling.

"Well, it's still early in the day, love," Mrs. Nealy spoke softly, holding Maximillian close to her bosom. "Maybe today will be different," she whispered, gazing out hypnotically, reflecting on her gardens waning beauty.

A patch of sunlight fell upon the windowsill. Mrs. Nealy thought about the many mornings she and Maximillian shared over her morning cup of tea on the front terrace. It was as though the sunlight was calling to her. As though the overpowering sweetness of the budding rose garden was inviting her into the unknown.

"At least we don't have to worry about cutting the grass," she mused to herself before being startled from her thoughts by a car traveling down Grove Street. Mrs. Nealy stared inquisitively at the vehicle. She knew everyone on the block and did not recognize the auto or the driver.

As the automobile moved closer, a large Rottweiler bounded from out of nowhere, startling the driver and causing the vehicle to swerve slightly to one side. Mrs. Nealy looked horrified. The dog was huge, the largest Rottweiler she had ever seen. His blood-red eyes and foaming drool made his presence even more menacing. As the dog hurled itself after the car, the driver adjusted his steering wheel and quickly sped down the roadway. The Rottweiler followed close behind the vehicle, lunging into its rear bumper.

Mrs. Nealy pressed her face against the windowpane to get a final glimpse of both the vehicle and dog as they faded into the distance. Speaking in a whisper as she continued to caress Maximillian, "He should have killed him. He should have rammed that dog with his car and killed him."

Maximillian let out a soft groan as Mrs. Nealy's caress grew tighter around him.

"Oh, I'm sorry, my darling," she said as she relaxed her hold on Maximillian. Maximillian tilted his head and looked up at her as if he could understand her every word.

"I don't mean to scare you," Mrs. Nealy continued,

"God knows how scared I am. You probably think I am a little nutty, Maximillian. Maybe I am. Maybe we all are."

It was not the first time she was frightened by the Rottweiler. It was about six months ago when the colossal dog first appeared. No one knew whose dog it was or how it found its way to the neighborhood. Mrs. Nealy stroked Maximillian's brow gently as she drifted back in thought to that first day.

Margaret Lawson's seven-year-old son Jimmy was playing outside when the dog came out of nowhere. Mrs. Nealy could only embrace the terror Jimmy must have felt when he looked up into the dog's growling face. It was a dreadful sight, Jimmy lying there all chewed up, near death. Margaret Lawson's cries drenched the entire neighborhood. The police searched the community for days. People from animal control and the local pound tried to help, but there was no sign of the Rottweiler. The dog had simply vanished.

Nine weeks passed before Jimmy left the hospital. The

right side of his body mangled, and he'd lost an entire outer ear.

"Poor child. He will be facing surgery in the future… at least he is alive," she said, sighing deeply while placing Maximillian back onto the windowsill.

"A penny for your thoughts," she whispered to Maximillian as she turned away from the window. "Breakfast will be ready in a moment, my love," she said as she headed toward the kitchen door. She Paused just short of the kitchen. Her mind raced back into the past to Angela Cassell.

Angie had been delivering mail to Grove Street for years. She was a pleasant, friendly woman. She'd raised two kids alone after her husband left her several years back. The rumor on the block was that he ran away with a younger woman. Except you would never have known that to be the case if you knew Angie. She was a short, dumpy little woman, but she was one of the happiest women Mrs. Nealy had ever known. Come rain or shine. Angie was always on the job until that morning. It was precisely one day after Jimmy arrived home.

"It was so strange," the words escaping quietly as Mrs. Nealy remained consumed in thought.

After little Jimmy's was attacked, there was no sign of the Rottweiler. Weeks passed, and the neighbors had gone back to their regular routines.

That morning, Angie knocked on the door of the old man's house. She always took the time to put the mail right into his hands. He was nearing his eighty-fourth birthday and was wheelchair-bound because of his weak legs.

Old man Elliot was the first house on the block to install synthetic grass. Everyone was so amazed at how beautiful and real it looked. Soon after, the Jacobs installed the grass on their lawn front, and slowly everyone followed. Grove Street looked lovely from the outside.

Such a nice old man thought Mrs. Nealy.

"You always wanted to hug him, or maybe it was him wanting to hug you," she mused. Old man Elliot looked forward to those brief moments with Angie.

Elliot lit up like a kid anticipating Christmas morning whenever she came his way. Like always, they chatted a bit on his rotting wooden porch before she headed off down his walkway to continue her route.

Angie stopped briefly to wave goodbye to Mr. Elliot, still seated in his wheelchair behind his screen door. As she turned away to continue, her path was blocked. It was as though the Rottweiler had materialized from out of nowhere right before her.

Angie jolted from surprise, dropping the bag of mail she carried at her side. Old man Elliot saw it all. He said Angie looked like a pale ghost, standing there staring down at the dog. She nearly ran but managed to stop herself, realizing there was not enough time or enough room between her and the dog, and she knew she would never make it back to the house. Plus, she didn't want the old man to get hurt.

Old man Elliot said that she nearly screamed, except time did not allow the sound to pass from her lips. The dog leaped forward into her chest, knocking her down onto her back. Her head struck the pavement with such force as the Rottweiler sank his teeth into Angie's neck, ripping it apart in quick movements. Elliot said, her head tilted in his direction, and he could see her eyes. She appeared to stare back at him before uttering the grimacing sounds that are made right before death. Elliot said he would never forget the look on her face, at that moment, before she died. He could feel her terrible pain at that very moment. Old man Elliot said he would feel that pain for the rest of his life.

The police were out searching the neighborhood within minutes after getting the call. There was no trace of the Rottweiler.

The entire community was frightened, yet, curiously, no one located outside of Grove Street ever reported seeing the dog. We were all mystified.

Old man Elliot blamed himself, even though we all told him that it was not his fault. He was immobile and lucky to be alive.

"What could an old man who couldn't walk do?" Mrs. Nealy asked herself aloud.

The next day, old man Elliot was found dead in his wheelchair with a shotgun across his lap, still sitting behind the screen door. His death listed as heart failure, except Ms. Pruett, from across the street, said she looked out the window at about 2:00 a.m. the morning after Angie's death. She said she could see the old man sitting in his wheelchair behind the screen door like he was watching for Angie. Like he was waiting for the dog to return. He was just sitting there waiting and watching the night.

Ms. Pruett said it was fear that stopped Mr. Elliot's heart. It was fear that killed him.

"Old man Elliot told me he could see the pain in Angie's eyes," Mrs. Nealy recalled Ms. Pruett saying. *"That he could probably feel her pain when he died."*

Since that time, Mrs. Gessler's dog Peanut had been attacked, chewed to death up the street, as was Mr. Steinberg's twelve-year-old springer spaniel, Skippy. No one lets their pets out anymore. No one goes out by themselves anymore either.

Maximillian turned toward the kitchen as the murmur of the electric can opener drew his attention. He knew breakfast would be ready soon. He turned his focus back to the bird in the weeping willow tree as it raised its wings and glided gently across the lawn. Suddenly Maximillian jumped, letting out a loud trill-like shriek, as the Rottweiler bounded out of nowhere, throwing itself upon the bird, snatching it out of mid-flight. The bird tried to escape, to fly, to raise itself in the air. The birds' effort was in vain.

The Rottweiler appeared to smile, pulling back his lips, catching sight of Maximillian in the window. Blood oozed from its mouth. His irregular jerking slowed as he stared fixated at the cat on the sill. A low, bellowing growl could be heard beneath the bird's shredded remains as the Rottweiler held it in his mouth before allowing it to drop lifeless to the ground. The dog's mouth opened wide, and the sun shone like little mirrors reflecting between sharp blood-stained teeth that formed a sardonic grin. His expression was defiant, taunting. The dog appeared to send out an ominous warning to Maximillian. It was as though his eyes were saying... *You're next.*

Maximillian arched his back and hissed vehemently, barely able to raise himself on trembling legs. He sensed evil. He felt the danger. Maximillian would never sit on the windowsill of Mrs. Nealy's house again.

That night the warm wind wailed through the trembling leaves of the weeping-willow, like a low cry. The lights in the windows on both sides of the street began to dim and fade one by one. The neighborhood was silent and still.

Sometimes you can hear the sobs of the frightened against the dark when the shadow of the Rottweiler looms over the little community on Grove Street. Some people say it is a mythical figure like in a dream or nightmare. Some say it is a curse. Others simply say it is the end of the world. There are no answers tonight. There is only fear.

4

BROKEN

Bertha, a baby-faced fourteen-year-old with round dimpled cheeks, whimpered softly under her breath. At the same time, her mother verbally berated her while roughly adjusting Bertha's hair and clothing.

"Look at you! Just like your father, a fat, ugly, miserable man. I guess there is nothing I can do about that, but I can control what you eat. Salads only from here on out, salads only," her mother said.

"You will not be both fat and ugly!" She continued sarcastically, "This is the best I can do. I don't have much to work with."

Bertha retreated to the bathroom, where she stood sobbing in front of the mirror. Her brown eyes swollen from the tears. Bertha was an average build, perhaps a little curvy for her age, but she was not more than ten pounds overweight. She was ordinary, but not ugly.

Bertha suddenly began slapping herself in the face repeatedly.

"I hate you! I hate everything about you," before picking up a hairbrush and striking the mirror. The glass cracked. Bertha cried harder, knowing she would receive more harsh berating once her mother discovered the broken mirror.

Over the next ten years, Bertha worked to erase the memories of her mothers' cruel treatment.

The sound of birds chirped in the trees that lined a tranquil, lightly clouded sky. Seated on a park bench, Bertha loved to spend her 60-minute lunch break at the park just up the street from her job. She was thinner now and had grown into a plain but somewhat attractive young woman.

As she glanced above into the drifting clouds while taking a bite of her sandwich, she was hit directly in the face with a balloon filled with water. The water-balloon stung as it burst and splashed her. Her face and hair wholly drenched, along with her crisp white blouse and her checkered skirt. Dropping her jaw and sandwich, she gasps loudly, stunned from the sudden attack as tears welled up in her eyes. Loud, youthful laughter, along with retreating footsteps, are heard in the background.

Still gasping, Bertha scrambled to locate a napkin or tissue in her purse. Unable to find anything dry, tears continued to flow from her eyes. Glancing up from her bag, a glare of sunlight bounced off Alicia, who was suddenly standing in front of her. Alicia extended a handful of wadded tissues toward Bertha.

Alicia appeared angelic through the glare of the sun.

"Here, let me help you," Alicia said as she sat down beside Bertha. She gently took Bertha's chin into her hand and glided the tissue across Bertha's face. Alicia was a classically beautiful young woman in her early 30s.

"Thank you. This happens to me a lot."

"What do you mean?" asked Alicia.

"I, I don't know. I guess I just seem to have a lot of bad luck."

"Luck? Some things don't have anything to do with luck; they just happen."

Bertha stared curiously at Alicia, not particularly understanding her reply as Alicia continues to wipe her face. Alicia's rubs grew harder.

"Ouch!" Bertha winced. Alicia stops wiping.

"Sorry, sometimes I can be a little heavy-handed."

"That's okay." Bertha smiles with reverence. Alicia continues to wipe.

The following day was a Saturday. Bertha was off on the weekends. She was relieved after having to return to work embarrassed by her drenched appearance. Still, she was excited to be meeting up with Alicia once again. They met at a restaurant suggested by Alicia. Bertha was excited to try out a new place and to be in the company of Alicia. They giggled together as they awaited the arrival of their lunch.

"Thank you, Alicia," said Bertha.

"Thank me for what?"

Bertha hunched her shoulders. "Uhh... For being so nice."

"You're a lovely person Bertha. You just have to remember that."

Bertha smiled as Alicia continued, "I just hope you feel better than you look!"

Stunned, Bertha thought Alicia's voice sounded strangely like her mothers.

"Huh! What did you say?" Bertha's voice was laden with concern.

The waiter arrives, distracting the two. He places large salads down in front of them both.

"Dig in. I'm telling you; you will love this salad. Healthy, delicious, plus we both can afford to drop a few pounds, don't you think?" Alicia said.

Bertha was taken aback by the thought of having heard her mother's voice and could not hear Alicia rattle on in the background. Instead, she brushed away her confused thinking and focused on her unappetizing salad.

Bertha's bedroom is brightly lit and colorfully decorated. Alicia sorted through a pile of clothing spread across the bed, carefully assessing each piece. Bertha and Alicia had become close since their meeting at the park a few weeks back.

"Here, try this blouse on. It will go good with that skirt," said Alicia.

After Bertha replaced the blouse she was wearing, Alicia pulled and tucked at Bertha's waist before stepping back to inspect Bertha's appearance. Alicia hikes up Bertha's skirt, exposing her knees. Bertha blushes.

Over the coming weeks and months, their visits together became more routine. On this night, Alicia sat on the bed, facing Bertha as she applied red polish to Bertha's nails.

"Ugh... I, I don't know if I like this," pulling her hand away. "It's so red," said Bertha.

Alicia paused momentarily, maintaining a firm grip on Bertha's hand. She looks closely at Bertha's nails and abruptly released her hand.

"You're right... we don't want you to look like a whore now, do we?"

Bertha's eyes widened at the comment as Alicia began to jokingly chuckle while tightening the lid on the red nail polish. She placed the polish beside a steel nail file lying on the bed.

Realizing that Alicia was making a joke, Bertha smiled and said softly, "Thank you, Alicia."

"There you go again, thanking me."

"I can't help it. You've been such a friend. These past few months have been wonderful. I feel like it's the start of a whole new life."

"Well... maybe it is," Alicia remarked, leaning over and flicking Bertha's hair behind her right ear.

"Okay... so what can we do with this hair?"

Alicia placed her hands on Bertha's shoulders and gently turned her towards the mirror. Bertha stared ahead into the mirror as Alicia tousled her hair before picking up the hairbrush beside her. She began to stroke Bertha's hair. The brush strokes were vigorous, forcing Bertha's head to jerk forward and backward repeatedly. Bertha squirmed with each stroke. As Alicia continued, Bertha's flinching head bobbled even more forcefully.

Bertha's gaze shifts to her eyes widening to an awkward stare at her reflection, a reflection that seems to draw closer and closer to her with each harsh brush stroke.

"Oh my god, your hair is disgusting. What are we going to do with it?" Alicia remarked as she continued to brush.

Suddenly, the sound of Bertha's mother's voice replaced Alicia's.

"Mange dogs' hair looks better than this. Disgusting. Hold still!"

Bertha's mother's face replaced Alicia's. She felt her mother slapping the side of her head.

"I won't tell you again." Bertha's mother's voice continued, "You're a mess. A fat ugly, useless mess!"

A paralyzing fear began to overtake Bertha. As tears gathered in her eyes, the sound of her mother's voice grew louder.

"Stop it! Just stop it! Sniffling and sniveling will not make a difference. You're just like your father. You're just like him, and you'll always be like him."

The creases across Bertha's forehead begin to deepen. Her eyes grew sizably larger, as did her anger, and she no longer felt in control of herself, growing angrier and angrier at her mother's words.

"I hate you, mother!" Bertha said, sobbing loudly.

Bertha grabbed the nail file on the bed. Tightening her grip, she began to slash Alicia over and over. Alicia screamed as Bertha wielded the large steel nail file, stabbing, striking, and repeatedly cutting at Alicia.

The light was dim in the hospital room as Nurse Jenny leaned over the young woman checking her heart rate. A second nurse examines the bandages covering her face and upper torso. Nurse Jenny jots notes on a clipboard.

A woman enters the room carrying a flower holder filled with roses. Nurse Jenny nods at her as she enters the room. "She's unresponsive at this time, so please, if you can keep your visit brief," said Nurse Jenny.

Both nurses exit as the woman places the vase on the bedside tray. Startled at what reminded her of a mummy wrapped in layers of bandages and gauze, she sits on the bed's edge and caresses a warm but lifeless hand.

"I'm so sorry... I didn't mean it. Please forgive me."
At that moment, Bertha drifts back to her apartment.

She stands in front of a cluttered dresser. Weary, blank eyes stare back from the mirror. She leans in closer, her nose only inches away. Startled by her own reflection, she blinks abruptly to clear away the fear confusing her. She pulled out a small photo frame from the top drawer. Tears spill out as she looks down at the photo.

"I hate you! I hate you! It's all your fault!" she cries out.

Her eyes suddenly reveal great rage. Bertha smashes the picture frame onto the dresser cracking the glass before tossing it to the floor. She sobs loudly at her reflection.

"You made me ugly… you did this to me!" Bertha closed her eyes tightly to avoid looking at herself.

"Why? Why do you hate me so much?"

Her eyes slowly opened. She is disoriented and confused by the contrast of light and warmth around her.

Am I conscious? Where am I? Why can't I move?

She is lying on her back, unable to move. Forced to stare into the white ceiling overhead—her mind moans, unable to speak.

A foggy image leans over into her view and gently touched her right wrist.

She becomes even more frightened as a second blurred figure comes into her limited line of sight. She feels excruciating pain as the hands move across her torso. Pounding aches reverberate throughout her body. She cries out in silent pain as her bandages are changed.

I can't breathe; her mind attempts to force the words out.

Help me, I can't breathe.

"I heard she did this to herself… and with one of those large nail files, can you believe it?" said Nurse Jenny to the second nurse continuing, "I feel like barfing just thinking about it."

"I know what you mean… crazy, isn't it?"

"Yeah, she's crazy. The doctor said she was delusional, split personality," said Nurse Jenny.

The second nurse shakes her head back and forth in disgust, a deep frown on her forehead.

"Paramedics found her in her bedroom, barely alive. Her screams were so loud, there were calls from several neighbors," said Nurse Jenny. She continued, "She even slashed her own throat. The doctor says her vocal cords are damaged, and she'll never speak again."

Bertha's body trembled as a glint of a tear appeared in the corner of her eye. Fear seizes her.

"Do you think she can hear us?" the second nurse asked.

"No. The body can make spontaneous movements when in a coma," responded Nurse Jenny, continuing, "Shhh, Bertha. Shhh. Breathe baby. Breathe."

Bertha flashes back to the park bench, where she wipes the water from the impact of the balloon from her face. Glancing up, the combination of the sun's reflection danced across the trees, creating movement. The laughter slowly vanished as three teens ran off in the distance. Bertha sat momentarily, wiping her face and brushing pieces of the balloon from her clothing before heading back to the office in her drenched attire.

Seated at a table on the restaurant patio, a waiter brings a large salad to the table. He muses as Bertha laughs and talks to the empty seat across from her. As he walked away, he chuckled under his breath, "I hope she leaves a double-tip." The room was dark, cluttered, and dingy. Bertha is seated on the bed painting her fingernails bright red. She raises her fingers and gently begins to blow at her nails. Stopping abruptly, Bertha glares at her nails before violently rubbing at the red polish. She picks up a steel nail file lying beside her and aggressively files away at the polish.

Suddenly stopping, Bertha catches her image in the mirror. Rising from the bed, Bertha steps inches from the mirror, still gripping tightly to the nail file, she stars trance-like into her own eyes.

"You're an ugly, disgusting whore!"

Bertha's voice was loud. Tears rolled down the sides of her face. As she gazed into the mirror, her mother's face replaced hers, the sound of her mother's voice rose loudly.

"You make sick! Look at you! Just look at you! You ugly, pitiful child!

Bertha screamed as she slashed and stabbed at her face and neck. Blood splatters as she cuts herself over and over, thrashing around the room. Her harrowing screams fill the air.

Startled from her thoughts by Nurse Jenny's voice, "She's unresponsive at this time, so please, if you can keep your visit brief."

A large vase of roses drifts into Bertha's view. A hand reaches out and takes Bertha's bandaged hand with a deliberate grip squeezing tightly. Bertha's silent gasps intensify at the recognition of her mother's voice.

"Look at you. You stay away for years, and I get a call that you're here. I suppose you'll want my help now," Bertha's mother mumbles annoyingly. "Lord, I can imagine what you look like under those bandages."

Bertha heard an echoing chilling scream rise from her soul.

A sound so horrible, a sound that she only hears.
Back in her apartment, the cracked picture frame lay on the floor in the blood-filled bedroom. Engraved at the bottom was the word mother. Beneath the broken glass is Bertha's mother's photo, a mirrored image of an aged Alicia.

5

APGAR HOUSE

"I have to thank God that I didn't kill nobody's kid, 'cause I usta' say, I'm not coming out of this place empty-handed. I'm gonna always have my gun locked and ready!"

Tanda came to Apgar House-twenty-one days ago. Angry, defiant, suspicious, and determined not to let her guard down for anyone.

"Most of my life has been spent in youth authority or jail. I don't know how to be with people. I like keepin' to myself 'cause that's all I know. In jail, you had to be that way 'cause that's the way it was. I wasn't going to end up being anybody's property, nobody's bitch, know what I mean? I just wasn't. I'd kill somebody 'fore I let that happen."

Seven ladies were living at Apgar House, just under the state's maximum allowed without official licensing.

All were recovering alcoholics, some recovering from both alcohol and drugs. Two were convicted teen murderers, remanded to the halfway house after serving time in lockup. They all looked the part; worn out, damaged teeth, rubbery skin, and sagging eyes. They had gone to hell and back, and hell again. Apgar was their last and only hope.

Today was the first time Tanda felt she could speak to the group. Tanda wanted nothing to do with the recovery house upon her arrival and little contact with its residents. She told herself that she was not like them, but she was. In truth, as she glanced at the faces of the women forming the circle with her, they were mirror images of herself.

"Do you still feel like killing somebody, Tanda?" asked Ms. Norma.

"Don't mess with me. I won't mess with you!"

"Oh, you bad," said Brenda. "I guess we're supposed to be scared."

"That's enough, Brenda," chimed Ms. Norma, who was also seated in the circle. "We're going to end our session this evening. I need each of you to think about positive things you will do to move forward in your lives. Be prepared to share with the group in our next session."

At twelve years old, Tanda walked fifty yards across the street to the neighborhood convenience store and pulled a gun on the owner in a desperate cry for attention.

"Give me your money now," she demanded, pointing the weapon she had stolen from her mother's bedroom directly at him.

At first, the merchant laughed, having known Tanda as the little girl from across the street. When he realized that she was not joking, he became furious.

"I'm gonna tell your mama!" he said.

His refusal angered the already troubled Tanda even more than her mother's lack of care and love.

Tanda fired a shot at the merchant. The bullet grazed his right shoulder, flew past him, and shattered a nearby windowpane. He screamed as the blood gushed from his wound. Tanda fled the store running as fast as she could. She was charged with attempted murder at the age of twelve and remanded to youth authority, where she spent the next six years of her life.

At age eighteen, Tanda was released into the world, with nowhere to go. Her mother had long since moved away with no forwarding address, and she had no other family or friends. She turned to the streets for her survival. Selling her body and diminishing her pain with alcohol and drugs. She became a full-blown alcoholic destined to return to hell if she did not get the help needed. Today, at age twenty-eight, the support was court-mandated, and it took all she could muster up inside her to walk through the doors of Apgar.

During the first eleven days, Tanda kept mainly to herself. She never spoke in the group sessions, and she rarely listened. Her defense was to tune everything and everybody out. She would barely look up when the other women taunted or ridiculed her.

"What? You too good to talk to us?" mocked Brenda, who at age sixteen drowned her father in the back yard hot tub. He was an alcoholic who climbed into her bed every time he got drunk.

That night, after his drunken intrude with his only daughter, he went out to the back yard to unwind in the hot tub. That was his cigarette after the conquest. It was a mild summer night when he climbed into the hot tub in an inebriated state. It would be the last time Brenda would ever have to smell his rancid stench pressed against her body.

Brenda had been captain of her baseball team. Baseball was the only thing that kept her in school. It was her escape from home and her dad. That night she took her bat to her father's head. After he was knocked unconscious, his body slumped submerged in the hot tub. Brenda calmly washed her bat clean in the swirling water. Her hands lingered in the bloodied water for a moment. The heat felt good, and there was a relaxing calmness about her. After rinsing her bat clean, she climbed back into her bed and went to sleep.

The next morning, Brenda got up, showered, dressed, and went to school. That was the last day she ever played baseball.

"Uppity bitch," Brenda whispered, her taunting directed at Tanda.

Tanda ignored her while thinking, *Just don't put your hands on me, bitch.*

Apgar House was under the charge of Ms. Norma and Dr. Erickson. Dr. Erickson had worked with recovery houses for years. In the past, his halfway houses accommodated men; this was his first women's recovery home. He had overseen Apgar for the past six years and brought a lot of experience to the table. Norma Erickson was his wife.

Tanda often overheard the ladies whispering about Mr. Erickson; they called him the ladies' man out of Ms. Norma's earshot. A couple of the women giggled about how he wasn't much good in bed. He rubbed Tanda the wrong way, but Tanda didn't trust men much, either. None of them.

Tanda came to Apgar House with only the clothes on her back. Everything had to be provided to her down to her underwear. Tanda was a big girl, so many of the outfits available from donations did not fit her. After about a week, Ms. Norma noticed that Tanda stuffed herself into tight-fitting clothing and shoes that were constrictive.

It was a fairy tale day for Tanda. It started with a surprise trip to a local shopping mall. Ms. Norma took Tanda aside earlier that day and whispered to her, "Go get your shoes on and come with me. I'm taking you shopping."

Ms. Norma bought Tanda several outfits, including two pairs of jeans and matching tops. She even bought her a couple of dresses for church Sunday, where mandatory attendance was required. After trying on dresses, Ms. Norma took Tanda into the lingerie department.

"Pick out whatever bra you want, don't worry about the price." Tanda would never forget those words, and the day she could pick and choose from an assortment of colorful patterned bras. There were so many frilly, silk, laced, and padded. Tanda had never seen so many bras. She was a full-size 38B and rarely wore a bra to contain her ample bosom. So, she decided to pass on the padded bras, selecting a pretty one that provided firm support.

"Thank you, Ms. Norma. I haven't had a bra in four years. We used to make them in jail, tie a ripped towel, or bedsheet around our titties, and we were good to go."

Ms. Norma was a harsh taskmaster. She didn't play, she was kind and caring to a point, but she didn't take no mess. If you didn't follow the rules, she'd ship you back to the county jail or simply open the front door and say, "Oh, you have a choice! The front door is right there. That crack in your ass can be split twice!"

She would tell you to get the hell out and fend for yourself in a hot minute. But, for some reason, Ms. Norma took a liking to Tanda. She could see that Tanda was a lost soul. And it was like she wanted to help her find herself.

Three days after her shopping trip with Ms. Norma, Tanda began to feel more comfortable. It was on this day that she opened herself up and shared with the group. She began to trust Ms. Norma. Tanda never trusted anyone before. She wondered if Ms. Norma knew about Dr. Erickson's extracurricular activities.

Once Tanda started to share with the other ladies, she learned more about many of the women who had come to Apgar House. And how a few had taken off during the night and never seen again. Some even managed to overdose from drugs, at least those were the rumors going around. No one saw anyone escape into the night or even die. They just woke up, and they were gone.

"Yeah, there was Cheryl, Sandra, Rosalyn, Marie." The list seemed to go on. "We were shocked about Cheryl, she had been clean for months, and we all thought she was gonna make it," said Angela.

"Why? She wasn't nothing but a dope fiend, just like you!" remarked Brenda nastily. "Just like all of us! Relapsing ain't nothing new, and Apgar sure in hell ain't no picnic!"

Angela had been at Apgar House for about fifteen months. She was a coke addict who wore a strawberry tattoo over her belly button. Her pimp Razor put it there to let the world know this woman is a whore that would do anything for drugs. His street name was tattooed right below the strawberry, so the johns would understand that she was his whore and that they best not mess with his money. That was his trademark, a strawberry with the word 'Razor' right below it. All of his whores were branded that way, except Angela also wore another of his well-known markings. A deep scar across her left cheek from a jagged-edged switchblade, a gift from Razor, for not bringing home enough cash one night. Razor didn't play either, and Angela never forgot. It was a reminder every time she peered into a mirror.

"We were upset when we got up that morning to find that Cheryl had overdosed during the night. Everybody was surprised, even Ms. Norma," Angela continued.

"It ain't like all of you been clean all the while you been here. You know you've been sneaking a little taste now and then," said Brenda.

That night, as Tanda lay in the darkness trying to sleep, she thought about how comfortable Apgar House was beginning to feel. Ms. Norma ran a pretty tight ship, and she was routine with her house checks, rarely leaving a stone unturned.

How was Cheryl able to smuggle her drugs into the house? Except, Brenda was right. "I am an addict."

Now and then, Tanda hungered after that euphoric feeling of crack pulsing through her veins. It was like taking a trip to heaven for a short while.

If I wanted it bad enough, I could figure out a way to get it here. After all, this ain't a real prison, Tanda thought. "And I knew how to get the drugs in prison, no matter what the guards tried to do to stop us," she mumbled aloud.

"Dr. Erickson, what a jerk," the words passing her lips quietly.

If it is true what the girls are saying about him, if I was desperate, I could give him a little taste of my cookie and then blackmail him with a sexual harassment lawsuit. I could even threaten to tell Ms. Norma in exchange for some drugs. That's that crack talking. I can't do that to Ms. Norma, her final thought before drifting off to sleep.

Over the next few weeks, Tanda became closer to many women at Apgar House and even closer to Ms. Norma. Ms. Norma would take Tanda out frequently, and during the weekly group therapy sessions, would talk about how well Tanda was doing. Tanda even enjoyed going to church Sundays and listening to the spirited sermons. More so, she looked forward to exchanging glances and smiles with a handsome young deacon, who seemed to take a liking to her.

A few months passed, and things were going quite well for Tanda. She was settling in at Apgar House and feeling a lot better about herself and life, in general.

Tanda never felt her mother's love and looked at Ms. Norma like the mother she never had. Ms. Norma made Tanda believe that there might be a future for her one day.

The next morning, the ladies woke to Angela's gut-wrenching screams. They were all told to stay in their rooms until further notice. Later that morning, Dr. Erickson called everyone together and announced that he had some terrible news. Tanda died during the night from what appeared to be an epileptic seizure.

Angela found Tanda on the floor of the downstairs bathroom. Her eyes frozen open, her body contorted in a frigid convulsed state. Foam spilled from her mouth.

The house reeled from gossip and speculations. Angela was nonstop about how she just could not believe it.

"You know it wasn't no seizure. Tanda was a drug addict, just like the rest of us," said Brenda.

"I just knew she was going to make it! I mean, there was Cheryl, Sandra, Rosalyn, Marie, oh hell no, and now Tanda. I just can't believe it!" said Angela.

Ms. Norma was also in a state of disbelief as she moved about Apgar, trying to be routine and focused. During the past six years, Ms. Norma lost a handful of young ladies to the streets or drugs, but Tanda was special. She worked extra hard and had been very hopeful that she could turn her around. It was hard to believe that Tanda had fooled her all along.

The loud knock on the door startled Ms. Norma out of her thoughts. She opened the door to a uniformed sheriff standing beside a frayed young woman, mandated by the courts to Apgar House. There was the smell of alcohol on her breath. The young woman was apprehensive and uncertain about how she would be received. Ms. Norma had been expecting her.

"Hello. Mrs. Erickson, I'm Sheriff Collins."

"Yes, please come on in. I've been expecting you."

After signing off on the paperwork, Ms. Norma thanked Sheriff Collins. She watched him pace off down the walkway back to his vehicle. Ms. Norma turned to look at the young woman.

"I have two things I need to say to you. The first is, welcome to Apgar House. The second is that I hope you enjoyed that beer I am smelling on your breath because it better be your last!"

During group therapy that afternoon, Ms. Norma formally introduced the new member of Apgar House to the ladies. She then spoke about how not to give up or lose hope.

"If you feel you need to talk, please know that I am here. It's never so bad that you need to resort back to the drugs or alcohol."

She also talked about Tanda. As she spoke, you could hear the difficulty she was having trying to hold back her pain and an overwhelming sense of failure. Ms. Norma had grown quite fond of Tanda. She thought about her broad smile and the last time she sat between her and Mr. Erickson on church Sunday.

"Now, I want you all to be nice to this young lady and help her along. I don't want to see another one of you be defeated by drugs ever again."

At the end of the session, Ms. Norma reminded everyone to finish up their daily chores before going behind closed doors in private consultation with the newest Apgar resident.

Brenda was one of the first women to move into Apgar six years ago. Apgar turned out to be a blessing for Brenda. It saved her life, and she found a mother in Ms. Norma. Brenda never knew her mother. Her father had stolen her away when she was a baby, at least that is what she told herself, never knowing the real story.

After killing her father, Brenda fantasized about her mother. She became obsessed with wondering who she was and dreaming about whether they both looked alike. When she came to Apgar, Ms. Norma was so kind and caring; she was the mother she had always missed in her life.

Brenda had a rough go upon first arriving at Apgar, but Ms. Norma took such good care of her. Brenda received so much love and attention that she did everything Ms. Norma asked of her, even remaining sober.

After two years of sobriety, Ms. Norma suggested Brenda be released; but she did not want to go. Apgar had become her home.

Once back out in the world, Brenda was unable to make a life on her own. She could not stop thinking about Ms. Norma; she craved the continued love and attention. Brenda wanted to go back home, back home to Apgar House.

When Brenda relapsed into drugs, she ended up back at Apgar, back home with Ms. Norma. But things were different, there were many more ladies in the home who also wanted Ms. Norma's attention, and Brenda grew increasingly jealous. She wanted all of Ms. Norma's love and could not bear the thought of sharing it.

Brenda mumbled under her breath while completing her chores. She carried a large trash bag through the house, emptying the smaller cans of trash into it.

"Ms. Norma never took me shopping. I never got new clothes, only hand-me-downs. Had to listen to Tanda talk about that damn bra all night!"

After locking the door behind her in her room, Brenda hurriedly lifted the carpet in the corner of the closet and pulled up a small floorboard. A plastic bag with several syringes lay hidden beneath the floor, along with three tightly sealed vials.

Reaching in, she pulled out a soiled disposable plastic syringe beside the plastic bag. Only a residual of the pure powdered cocaine and lemon juice cocktail remained in the barrel of the tube. She wondered when Ms. Norma would be going back to the grocery store. They were out of lemon juice and vinegar, and she wanted to make sure they were on the grocery list. Injecting vinegar or lemon juice with a pure powdered cocaine base was nearly always fatal, especially if you pushed the plunger in a millimeter too far. Two of the vials were low on lemon juice and vinegar; the third was nearly full of cocaine.

Wrapping the syringe carefully in some toilet paper pulled out of the trash bag, Brenda placed it deep inside the plastic garbage bag.

As she tossed the trash bag into the outside bin, she thought about the new girl behind closed doors with Ms. Norma.

"Oh, I'll help her along," she said. "I'll help her like I helped all the others. Ms. Norma is my mother. She's mine."

6

SHADOW

Wellington, the next-door neighbor's dog, was loose again, mischievously scurrying around, sniffing along the edges of the lawn before bounding onto the grass next to the rose garden. A small, wrinkled, monkey-faced pug, Wellington lowered his weight onto his hind legs and positioned himself into a squatting position.

"Ar-owl," a sudden, painful yap burst from the dog as he quickly bound from the yard setting aside any thought of relieving himself. Only soft whimpers trailed behind him.

Nine-year-old Eric Stark roared with laughter as he lowered his BB gun and proclaimed, "Bull's-eye!"

Eric was big for his age and carried twenty pounds over what was considered an average weight for his size. He was an ordinary-looking boy, unadorned and plain with dirty brown hair and thick hairy eyebrows. His T-shirt appeared one size too small and hugged his waistline. A slight glimpse of belly peaked from between the hemline of his shirt and beltline.

Crouched behind the tree in his front yard, Eric awkwardly raised himself to a stand and brushed the dirt off his knees. Eric tried twice before to clip Wellington with his BB gun but missed on both occasions. He was proud of today's accomplishment.

"I bet he won't be back," he said, chuckling under his breath as he turned and headed toward the front door of his house.

Inside, he walked into the dining room, where his mother was setting the table for dinner.

"Can I have a cookie?" He said, strolling past his mother into the kitchen.

"No, wait until after dinner, your dad is on his way, and dinner will be ready in fifteen minutes," she replied loud enough so that Eric would hear her.

"Okay," he said, as he reached into the cookie jar, took two cookies, and headed towards his bedroom on the upper level. He ate the cookies as he climbed the stairs and entered his bedroom, located at the hall's end.

The room was dimly lit, with dark blue window coverings with oversized images of cartoon comic heroes. Eric flipped on the wall switch that turned on the table lamp next to his bed. His shadow illuminated the wall of his bedroom.

Eric was a bully. He was bigger than his classmates. Bullying was his way of making himself feel superior and not admitting his secret envy of them. He never really liked the fact that he was fatter than everyone else. He hated feeling ordinary. He enjoyed terrorizing the others and thought of himself akin to the comic book superheroes on his curtains. He called himself the *Intimidator*, a super-villain oppressor.

"Eric, Eric! Dinner is ready," called his mother from downstairs twenty minutes later. As Eric started to exit his room, he took a quick look to his right. He thought he caught a slight glimpse of movement in the corner of his eye. There was nothing. He bolted down the steps.

The next day at school, the Intimidator was up to his usual behavior. He had already hit Robby in the eye, taken Derrick Johnson's lunch money, and nearly twisted Gerald Dawkins' arm backward.

The sun's heat felt like a hot sauna. Sweat rolled down Eric's face as he headed back to class after the lunch break. His shadow was dark and stretched across the ground as he walked. Right before he entered the building, he did a quick double-take and glanced down at his shadow. He felt ill at ease for a moment, something was out of place, but he could not put his hand on it. He stepped into the school building.

In class, Eric sat near the window. Through the half-open blinds, the sun shone, causing the filtering light to reflect his shadow draped across his desk and reaching onto the floor. As he sat ignoring the words of the teacher's lecture, he glanced at the shadow. It moved. Eric looked closely at the shadow.

"What the..." he whispered under his breath. He held himself still, barely even breathing, and stared at his shadow. The shadow moved. Startled, Eric closed his eyes tightly before slowly reopening them to clear his head and refocus his eyes. He sat almost statue-like, holding his breath even longer, staring down at his shadow. The right arm of the shadow balled its hand into a fist and suddenly threw it in Eric's direction. Eric screamed, his body jerked to the left, causing him to fall out of the chair to the floor. The classroom broke out in wild laughter. Eric was too frightened to be embarrassed.

"What is it now, Eric?" said Mrs. Tennison, sarcastically.

"My shadow... My shadow moved!"

The classroom continued to roar in blustering laughter.

"Quiet down! Quiet down, class," shouted Mrs. Tennison.

Turning to Eric, she spoke in an annoyed tone.

"That's enough, young man. If you don't get off that floor and get back into your seat right now, you'll be visiting the principal's office."

"But..." uttered Eric.

Before he could continue, Mrs. Tennison raised her voice, harshly, "Get up now! Enough of your shenanigans!"

Eric pulled himself cautiously back into his seat, keeping a close watch on his shadow. Mrs. Tennison's voice seemed distant in the background, and Eric could barely hear the giggles from the classmates sitting nearby. He stared wearily at his shadow, watching as if he was on a stake-out waiting for the commission of a crime.

Eric's eyes remained glued to the shadow, barely blinking, never glancing away, until the sun shifted, and the shadow faded away.

That night at dinner, Eric tried to tell him mom and dad about the shadow.

"Cut it out, Eric! Stop playing around and eat your dinner. Look, I'm not in the mood for your foolishness tonight," said his dad.

"But Dad, it's true... my shadow moved," Eric spoke in a mild panic. "Dad, I promise, it did move!"

"Of course, it moved, Eric. That is what shadows do; they move with you," said his mother.

"But Mom, my shadow moved by itself. It balled its fist up at me and tried to hit me!"

"That's it, go to your room! I've had it with you," his dad retorted. "You need to be trying to bring your grades up instead of making stupid remarks!"

"Honey, don't be so harsh."

"Maybe if you stop babying him and spoiling him so much, he might start acting like he has some sense!"

Eric shoved his seat back forcibly and angrily vaulted from the table.

"Wasn't hungry anyway!" he grumbled under his breath.

In his room, Eric sat quietly on his bed in the dark,

wondering what would happen if he turned on the light. He reached towards the lamp next to his bed and clicked the light switch on. For a moment, Eric was like a mannequin, frozen in place while his shadow swelled across the bedroom wall. The shadow seemed unusually large, rising to the edge of the ceiling. It began to move towards him. Eric was petrified. He yanked at the lamp, knocking it over as he quickly turned off the switch.

Eric did not move; and did not sleep that night. He lay in complete darkness with his head beneath the covers.

The next day at school, Eric looked disheveled and on edge. He had run to school trying to out-pace his shadow. But every time he looked down, his shadowy silhouette was right beside him, moving in a ridiculing motion. It was as if his own shadow was poking fun at him. As he ran, his shadow seemed to skip alongside him.

In class, Eric made such a ruckus when Mrs. Tennison opened the window blinds to let in the sunlight; Eric ended up in the principal's office.

Robby was floored with laughter, still wearing the black eye resulting from the blow he received from Eric just the day before.

In the school office, Eric sat waiting for his parents to arrive. He sat in a chair next to the door just outside the principal's office. His shadow stretched across the floor beside him.

"Leave me alone!" Eric shouted at his own shadow. "What do you want? Just leave me alone!"

The school secretary, who was seated at her desk nearby, peered over the rim of her glasses in Eric's direction, shaking her head.

"Damn shame," she said. "These kids get hung up on drugs real young nowadays. Just a damn shame," still shaking her head.

When his parents arrived, Eric could hear his dad speaking to the principal through the closed door.

"I don't know what's going on with him. He's been acting really silly these days, going through some strange puberty or something," his father spoke disturbingly.

"Mr. and Mrs. Stark, this behavior is nothing new; Eric has been the class clown, disruptive, and a troublemaker for a long time. He regularly bullies the other children, and this is not the first time I notified you of his prankishness and bad behavior."

"He's really a good boy," said Mrs. Stark.

"No, no, Mrs. Stark, he lacks discipline." The principal continued, "And now this nonsense about his shadow moving takes the cake. I'm not sure what to tell you both, but if his behavior does not change for the better, you will likely have to enroll him into another school."

At dinner, Eric's parents barely spoke to one another. Eric did not talk either; he just watched his shadow magnify beside him.

It was another restless night for Eric. He remained buried beneath his bed coverings in the blackened room, afraid of the dark but more fearful of what was in the light.

"Hurry up, Eric, you're going to be late for school," his
Mother said the next morning.

"I don't want to go to school today, mom. I don't feel
well."

"You're going to school, boy," barked his father.

As Eric stepped out onto the shaded front porch, the
morning sun glared down into the front lawn just a few feet
away from where he stood. He knew that as soon as he left
his porch, the sunlight would hit him, and his shadow
would appear.

"Get going, boy!" his dad yelled from the living room
window. "I told you to go to school!"

"Dad, please!"

"Son, I'm not playing with you. Don't test me," his father
angrily responded.

Eric took a deep breath and started running, looking
straight ahead. His breathing was labored as he raced past
blurred surroundings. Perspiring profusely, he ran
frantically down the street as his shadow grew massive and
more distorted beside him. An onset of apprehension and
despair engulfed Eric. He became more terrified as his
shadow swallowed up the entire sidewalk surrounding him.
Eric turned around quickly to race back to his home. As the
shadow loomed before him, it emerged and rose from the
ground in a menacing motion. The sound of Eric's scream
was horrific.

A few hours later, outside of Eric's home, Wellington, the
little monkey-faced pug from next door, scurried down the
sidewalk, cautiously sniffing the grassy lawn edges.

Remembering the sharp pain from his last visit near the rose garden, he decided not to venture onto the lawn. Instead, Wellington continued along the sidewalk, sniffing, smelling, before suddenly stopping abruptly on the pathway.

Wellington looked puzzled; his ears lay slightly back as he tilted his head, looking curiously down at the sidewalk. The dog stepped backward, stopped, and slowly crept forward, insidiously investigating the ground in front of him. He sniffed.

There was a large shadow stretched across the surface of the sidewalk. Wellington's ears stood straight up. A curious sound rose from the cement below his paws. It was a high-pitched, prolonged mournful cry. Wellington carefully sniffed at the surface of the shadow. Realizing that the vague semblance appeared to pose no harm to him, he lifted his right hind leg and peed on the faint, indistinct image. Stopping to sniff his newly-marked territory, Wellington yapped suddenly at what appeared to be panic-stricken eyes staring up from the center of the darkness. Frightened by the piercing, illuminating eyes gazing directly at him, Wellington quickly skirted down the sidewalk.

Eric Stark stared up in horror from within the shrouded darkness cast across the cemented surface. His face tormented as the shadow slowly faded with the vanishing sunlight.

7

DON'T MOVE

"Hands where I can see them! Put your hands where I can see them! Stop! Don't move! Stop!"

Several loud gunshots shattered the air. The scene turned to panic as neighbors awakened and spilled from their houses. Screams soon crowded the background as onlookers flowed into the street.

Officer Jason Reezi shouted over the car's radio scanner, "Shots fired. Shots fired! Officer needs assistance! Send back up!"

A group of people began to taunt the officer at the scene. "Murderer!"

"You killed him! You didn't have to kill him!"

"Death to the pig! Death to the pig!"

The following day Reezi sat nervously in Captain Foster's office after spending five hours with internal affairs. Reezi's incident report was spread open in front of the Captain.

"The public is riled up about this one. The media is reporting another black man killed by a white police officer. The good thing is you're a twenty-year veteran with a clean record."

"Yes, sir."

"I know you've been with Internal Affairs all morning, but I want you to tell me again how this all went down."

"Yes, sir," responded Reezi.

Reezi continued, "I spotted the sedan speeding down Harrison Drive. My radar gun clocked 35 in a 25-mile zone. I turned on my lights and siren and immediately followed in pursuit. While in pursuit, the driver tossed an item out of the passenger side window. The street was dark. I didn't notice where it landed due to large bushes lined along the several block stretch."

"Could you make out what was being thrown out the window?"

"It was small, white. It looked like a plastic baggie, sir."

"The dashcam doesn't show anything being tossed. You do know nothing was found?"

"Yes, sir. But I saw him toss something out the window, sir. It was dark and hard to see, but I know I saw something. There were a couple of people on the street, sir. Someone could have easily picked it up."

"Can you explain why your vest camera was not on?

"It happened so fast, sir. I didn't have time to activate it."

"Continue officer," said the Captain.

"From the PA speaker, I shouted to the driver to pull over now."

"And, again, why you didn't call for backup? "

"It happened so fast, sir. As soon as I was getting ready to call, fearing he wasn't going stop, he pulled over to the side of the road and stopped the car. After stopping, he quickly exited the vehicle and headed directly towards me."

Reezi took a deep breath before continuing.

"At that point, I pulled out my weapon and jumped out of the car, positioning myself behind the door. I yelled at him to stop, to stand down as I was jumping out of the vehicle. He continued toward me. That was when I yelled, "Hands, where I can see them! Put your hands where I can see them! Stop! Don't move! Stop!"

"Did he ever say anything to you?"

"Sir, I was yelling at him to stop. I didn't hear him say anything."

"What compelled you to shoot?"

"He was coming at me. He appeared angry, crazed. He reached behind his back. I thought he was reaching for a weapon. I shot!"

"How many times did you release your firearm?"

"I think about 5-6 times, sir."

"It was 6 times, officer. He had 6 bullets in him."

"Yes, sir."

"Could you have avoided deadly force?"

"I believe the shooting was justified. I believed the driver was going for a gun. I believed my life to be in danger, sir."

"But there was no gun."

"No, sir, it turns out he was reaching for his cell phone."

"Not sure why he jumped out of the car... why didn't he just stay in his car?" Captain Foster appeared to be asking himself.

"I don't know, sir," responded Reezi.

"How's your wife, Officer?" asked Captain.

"She's as good as can be, sir."

"Good," Captain Foster paused a moment before continuing. "While I wait for the final report from internal affairs, you will be assigned to desk duty for the next two-three weeks."

"I understand, sir."

Reezi remained seated in the patrol car in his driveway. A physically fit man of forty-years, the grey sprinkled throughout his hair was due more to the stress in his life rather than age. His eyes wearied after the long day of interrogation by internal affairs.

Reezi opened his glove compartment and pulled out a small pocket-sized notebook and a few loose papers. Before entering his house, he tossed the book and paper-fragments into the trash can sitting curbside in front of his house.

After entering the home, Maria, his wife's caregiver, greeted him.

"Hello, Mr. Reezi."

"Hello, Maria. How is she?"

"She had a quiet day, sir. No incidents. She is still in and out. I try to keep her with her pain medication so she does not suffer. The cancer is getting the best of her, but I try to make her as comfortable as possible."

"Thank you, Maria. That is all you can do."

"I'll be back at 7:00 a.m. tomorrow. I left your plate in the microwave and a salad on the table. You try to get some rest, Mr. Reezi."

"Thank you, Maria. I'll see you in the morning."

Making his way into the bedroom with his dinner plate and salad, he removed his uniform before clicking on the television. The sound was faint as the news was still reporting on the shooting and the calls for his firing by the victim's family and Black community leaders. Reezi's lack of appetite was uncommon, only taking a few bites of his meal.

Amelia was sleeping when Reezi walked over to her beside. Her hospital bed was in an adjoining room. He leaned over and kissed her gently on her forehead. She was as beautiful to him as ever, even in her battle with cancer. Her face was paling. A brightly colored bandana had replaced her once curly blond hair; her frame was thinner and more fragile. Amelia's once wide green eyes were now narrowed and weighted from the weariness of her condition. The brightness has gone from them, but Reezi did not care.

Jason Reezi loved Amelia from the first moment he met her nearly nineteen years ago, fresh out of the police academy. He fell in love with her cheerful disposition. Her personality radiated throughout. They married three months after meeting and have been together ever since.

Amelia prepared herself to face death; they both knew it was looming near. She chose to live her last days in her home, among her memories. Beside her sat a framed photo of their wedding. The walls contained many framed pictures of their travels over the years, Europe, Japan, Hawaii. Little artifacts of memories set all about the room.

They had no children, just each other, and her home was a place that she loved. Before her illness, she spent her days creating a warm and welcoming environment for her husband to come home to after his arduous days on the force.

Amelia opened her eyes.

"Hi," she spoke through a breathy whisper.

"Hi, honey," he responded. "Can I get you anything?"

Her voice scratchy, "Water."

Reezi reached over to the bedside table and picked up the glass of water, a thin plastic straw already protruding from it. He gently lifted her head slightly so she could take a sip.

"I love you," he said, as she closed her eyes and returned to deep sleep.

Two weeks later, Jason Reezi was exonerated of all complaints. Internal affairs concluded that his actions were found to be lawfully executed and that no policies were broken. The public was enraged at Captain Foster's press conference, indicating that no charges would be filed and that the shooting was determined to be justifiable. Reezi was relieved. He would be back on the job within the week.

Over the next two weeks, Amelia's condition worsened. She was weak and heavily sedated most of the time. Things were still rough on the job for Reezi; the community can be slow in forgetting, even slower in forgiving, if ever.

Reezi had arrived home after a long day.

"How's she doing, Maria?"

"Not so good, Mr. Reezi. I'm worried. Do you want me to stay over tonight?"

"No, Maria. I'll see you in the morning. I'll be close by her tonight."

"Please call me if you need me, have a good evening Mr. Reezi."

"Good night, Maria."

Jason followed his regular nightly routine placing his gun and badge on the dresser beside his dinner plate. Undressing out of his uniform and turning the TV on to Amelia's favorite game show. After finishing his meal, Jason entered the adjoining bedroom where Alicia slept. Her breathing labored with light wheezing.

Jason kissed her gently on the forehead. Sitting beside her, he slipped his hand in hers.

The TV played quietly in the background as the show host shouted, "Can we make a deal?"

Amelia's eyes thinly opened; her lips curled into a small smile. Suddenly, the TV stations breaking news theme sounds in the background, and a newscaster speaks.

"The family of victim Gerald Johnson, slain by Officer Jason Reezi, has filed a wrongful death civil lawsuit against the officer."

Jason started to rise from the bed; however, Amelia weakly grasped his hand. She listened.

"The family believes that there has been an injustice in the killing of Gerald Johnson, who they believe was murdered on his way home from work." The reporter continued. "The lawsuit seeks 5.2 million in civil damages, naming the police department, the city, and Officer Jason Reezi.

At that moment, Amelia tried to open her mouth to speak, but no words came out. Her dulled green eyes, surrounded by red broken blood vessels, appeared terrified. Jason pulled away from Amelia's hand and rushed to the TV. He clinched the remote tightly, pressing the off button. Clutching his hands to his face, Reezi drifted in thought.

Six months prior.

Amelia spent the past 30 days in the hospital, and Jason was preparing the home for Amelia's return. He wanted to make her stay as welcoming as possible during her last few months of life. The chemotherapy was a setback for her destroying some bone marrow. Her fever ran so high that the process had taken a toll on her entire body. The truth was that her doctor gave her approximately six months to live.

Jason's sole mission was to make her life over the next six months as comfortable as possible.

Looking for precious memories that he could place about the room, Jason found the key to her storage chest in the attic.

Digging through the photos of their marriage and years of memories, he smiled to himself. He spent hours reading through the birthday, anniversary, and holiday cards he had given Amelia. She even kept many of the cards she had given him. There were so many. His heart was overwhelmed, as the keepsakes reminded him even more of how easy it was to love her.

Jason had not always been the perfect husband. Two years ago, pressure from the job negatively impacted their marriage. He worked long hours, sometimes double shifts.

One night, he had a domestic abuse call. The young woman had been beaten by her husband. Her cries were so loud that the neighbors called the police. Upon his arrival, he found many of the neighbors had poured into the apartment complex hallway. He found the man's wife bloodied and bruised from the large gash opened above her lip. Her pink pajamas soaked in blood. Her two-year-old daughter cried loudly in the background.

Officer Reezi called for an ambulance and backup as he placed the husband in handcuffs. Without warning, he felt his back plunged by a deep piercing pain. He had been stabbed with a kitchen knife by the man's wife. Two of the neighbors looking on stopped him from being killed that night.

The stress of the continued arrests, the murder scenes, and crime had already impacted his marriage. But the disappointment in himself for not being more perceptive affected his personality and his relationship. It was nearly a year with counseling before he found himself again.

Reminiscing, as he flipped through his wife's keepsakes, Jason ran across a group of letters addressed to Amelia. None of the envelopes included a return address. Wondering if they might contain something that would be meaningful to Amelia, he started reading them. The letters were emotional expressions of love and lust. Jason trembled as he became fixated on specific words on the pages, 'kisses, wetness, body, love.' The letters signed in closing with 'Eternally yours' and a small hand-drawn heart.

Jason became enraged as he read the words. Finally, what appeared to be the last letter was a response indicating the agony the letter writer felt from Amelia's decision to end the relationship. *I love you, and I know that you love me too.* The words further indicated that the writer did not understand how she still loved Jason with his neglect and lack of attention.

"You deserve so much better," Jason muttered the words as he continued reading. "I will always be there for you if you ever need me. Your love," preceding the hand-drawn heart.

That last letter was dated after the end of Jason's counseling sessions when he realized that he had neglected his wife for nearly a year.

Jason spent the next hour crying. He loved Amelia and wanted to show her how much he loved her. Though he was increasingly infuriated at the thought of the other man, he searched her belongings and dug through every piece of paper in her possession until he found the name Gerald.

Gerald was an art curator at one of the local museums. He was a handsome, clean-shaven man with chocolaty smooth skin. At thirty-eight years old, Gerald was four years younger than Amelia. He magnified charisma with a smile so big that you could count his teeth.

Amelia started attending the museum regularly a few months after Jason's recovery from the stabbing. She spent many days alone at the museum, which had become a beautiful place of refuge for her. Amelia loved art. That was where she met Gerald.

She savored her regular museum visits and their conversations together. Gerald shared his knowledge of the art pieces, taking her behind the scenes of the museum, sharing his job, and how the beauty found its way to the gallery exhibits.

Amelia loved her husband, but over the months, she also fell in love with Gerald. Even without a name, the letters revealed a lot to Jason.

After arriving at the precinct the following day, Jason researched motor vehicle records. He searched for BMW owners with the name Gerald, including names beginning with the letter G. He recalled one of Amelia's letters referencing his purchase of a new BMW. The words *Amelia, I can't wait to take you for a ride*, stuck in his mind.

Officer Reezi searched every local museum for male curators whose name had Gerald or a G in it. It did not take long to match the curator, the BMW through DMV registration, and identify the person he was seeking. He had an address. He found Gerald Johnson.

As the soft moon lit the night, Jason sat outside of Gerald Johnson's house. He followed his every move for the next six months. Jason learned his routine. The time he went to work, the roads he traveled. Jason kept track of Gerald's movements in a small pocket journal he stored in his car's glove compartment.

A month ago, on the night of the shooting, Jason knew Gerald would be traveling along the secluded dark street. He often left the museum late at night when everyone along the path was long asleep.

Jason pulled Gerald's car over. He approached his car and asked for his license and registration.

"Why was I stopped, officer?" asked Gerald.

"Sir, I asked for your license and registration."

"I have them right here; I'd just like to know why I'm being stopped." While handing his license and registration over, Gerald's eyes met Officer Reezi's.

"Wait a minute, I know you. You're, you're Amelia's husband. You've been following me. I've seen your car. What in the hell is happening here?"

"You were going 35 in a 25-mile zone," Reezi responded forcefully.

"That's bullshit! You know I wasn't speeding."

"And you're right! I am Amelia's husband. It's about you touching my wife. It's about me killing you if you ever contact her again."

"Look, asshole; this is harassment."

"This is only the beginning if you don't heed my words," Jason replied cynically.

Gerald felt intimidated. He considered reporting Reezi, but he did not want to hurt Amelia. He still loved her.

Officer Jason Reezi wanted Gerald to see his face. He wanted him to feel fear.

"I'm going to let you off with just a warning."

"Yeah, right!" snapped Gerald starting his car up.

As Reezi started towards his police car, Gerald yelled out the window, "I see why Amelia came to me. You're full of shit, man." Gerald pulled off.

Enraged by Gerald's comment, Jason hurried to his car and followed closely behind him for the next six blocks. The police car lights flashed brightly behind Gerald as he grew more enraged by Jason's continued harassment, maintaining his 25-mile speed. Suddenly, the siren wailed. Furious, Gerald pulled over to the curb, stopped his car, and jumped out immediately, sprinting towards Officer Reezi.

"Look, man, you're acting like some kind of psycho."

"Hands where I can see them! Put your hands where I can see them! Stop! Don't move! Stop!"

Reezi's heart throbbed from the adrenaline racing through his body. He pictured Amelia in the arms of Gerald, and he became livid.

"I'm calling the police," Gerald shouted as he reached for his phone in his back pocket.

Six-bullets tore through Gerald's body. Reezi aimed directly at his temple; the first bullet shattered his head. Part of his scalp slipped away as blood splashed in all directions.

Gerald had no time to react, only to gaze wildly with the first strike. Before his limp body could touch the ground, five additional bullets struck him. Bloody spots soaked through his clothes like a grotesque tie-dyed pattern.

Jason's thoughts bringing him full circle, he hurried back to Amelia's bedside. Amelia's dull and swollen eyes stared up in horror at Jason. Tears rolled down her face.

Amelia knew Jason had discovered her affair. She knew Jason had murdered Gerald.

"I'm sorry... I'm so sorry, Amelia," he said as a soft moan escaped her lips. A look of great sadness and disbelief as she took her last breath. Jason, pained with grief, climbed in bed beside her, sobbing as he held her body tightly against his.

The news permeated with reports about Gerald Johnson's shooting the morning following the incident. Maria had arrived at the home at 7:00 a.m. Officer Reezi left shortly after her arrival for the meeting with Internal Affairs. Maria had tended to Amelia and was in the kitchen tidying up. She could hear the garbage truck down the street and quickly grabbed the kitchen trash bag to take out before they passed the house. Opening the bin, she noticed the small pocket journal.

Without a doubt, Maria was an excellent caregiver to Amelia, but her curiosity always got the best of her. She plucked the journal out of the can before tossing the trash bag into it. She wore a broad smile waving to the sanitation worker clinging to the side of the truck as it pulled up in front of the house.

Maria routinely snooped around the house. One day she discovered she was a part of Amelia's will. The Reezi's had no family or next of kin. This fact attracted them to one another, bringing them even closer together. In the event they both passed, fifty percent of their estate, including the home, would be left to Maria, the rest to charity.

For the next month, after discovering the journal, Maria kept Officer Reezi's secret to herself and went about her chores routinely. Amelia's condition was failing severely, and Maria sensed she might not last through the night. When Jason arrived home that evening, Maria greeted him as usual.

"How's she doing, Maria?"

"Not so good, Mr. Reezi. I'm worried. Do you want me to stay over tonight?"

"No, Maria. I'll see you in the morning. I'll be close by her tonight."

Maria left Jason's dinner in the microwave with a salad bowl on the table. Except, this time, she added an undetectable ingredient, one that would stop Jason's heart slowly after ingestion. After some research, Maria found that the plant root Aconite causes cardiac arrest. She ordered the plant on eBay from Asia.

When it arrived, she chuckled, speaking to herself, "You can buy anything on the internet."

Maria wore plastic gloves as she chopped up small pieces of the plant root into the mixed green salad, tossed with onion, tomatoes, bell pepper, and dried cranberry. She added red pepper flakes along with a tart vinaigrette sauce to hide the taste.

Arriving at her shift the following morning, Maria quickly removed the dinner plate, scrubbed it clean, dried it thoroughly before placing it in the kitchen cabinet. She washed any remaining salad down the garbage disposal and wiped down the area with cleanser and bleach. She called the police.

Captain Foster stood over the bodies. Amelia lay wrapped in the arms of Jason; they were like two angels embraced by love.

"What happened here?" asked the Captain.

The medical examiner responded, "Cancer got the best of her, Captain, and it looks like his extreme grief may have triggered a heart attack. He's wrapped around her tightly, and there are dried tear stains on his face."

"Sad day. He was one of our best," replied Captain. "It broke his heart when he learned she had cancer."

"Yes, he was a good officer, sir."

"Who found the body?"

"The caregiver. We were able to get her statement, but she's with the paramedics now. She was having rapid breathing. I think she was going into a mild-shock after finding them both," responded an officer on the scene.

"Have one of the officers drive her home. She doesn't need to be here."

"Yes, sir, Captain!"

8

PEEPHOLE

The room suddenly went pitch-black at about 11:00 p.m. in Joyce Calhoun's apartment, a private unit located at the end of a long corridor. The perfect location for Joyce, who had a genetic predisposition for panic disorders. Joyce was a manic-depressive agoraphobic. She lived in near solitude at the end of the hallway for the past ten years.

Her mother was introverted, and as a small child, Joyce was very bashful and shied away from meeting people. Growing up, she relished her isolation, staying away from large crowds and public gatherings.

Joyce began to sever all her social ties and became so

recluse that it concerned those that knew her. Her apartment sat hidden away from prying eyes and removed from the other neighbors.

An attractive, middle-aged woman, nearing her mid-fifties, her only outside visits came from Deacon Carter, who stopped by weekly to drop off groceries.

A longtime family friend, Deacon Carter, had known Joyce's mother and understood Joyce's condition. He recognized the seriousness of her isolation and frequently tried to talk Joyce into seeking treatment. He spoke about how her illness was treatable, but Joyce didn't want to discuss doctors or therapies. She didn't believe there was a problem and did not feel that she needed treatment. Joyce could not understand why Deacon Carter continued to waste time discussing the topic.

There is nothing wrong with me, she would always say to Deacon Carter when he broached the subject. *I just liked being by myself.*

She was perfectly contented with being away from people and outside the reach of the rest of the world. The solitary was a godsend to Joyce, though she did welcome the brief weekly visits from Deacon Carter.

The sudden darkness caught Joyce off guard, interrupting the end of the horror movie she had been watching from bed. She loved a good zombie, werewolf, or ghost story, which was ironic because Joyce hated the thought of real psychotics beyond her sequestered lifestyle.

Suddenly, there was a loud clamor coming from just outside her apartment. Joyce swung her legs over the edge of the bed. Her toes moved along the carpet, feeling for the fluffy worn animal slippers, which had become a regular part of her daily footwear. Locating them, she slid her feet into the slippers and made her way out of the darkened bedroom, moving cautiously toward the front door.

"Who's there? Who's out there?" she said, straining to position her eye closer to the peephole. "Who's out there?" she repeated, staring into the dimly lit corridor.

Joyce touched her hand to the doorknob. As her fingers wrapped around the cold polished brass knob, she felt a surge of panic with the thought of what might lie in wait on the other side of the door. Her heartbeat began to race as her palms became clammy with sweat. She quickly released the doorknob. Joyce had not ventured beyond her front door for several years. Even peering into the hallway through the peephole caused feelings of discomfort and distress. She wondered why the corridor appeared to be illuminated while her apartment remained utterly dark.

"Is someone there?" she called out. "Hello." *What is that?* She thought to herself. *Footsteps? Are those footsteps?* "Hello...Hellooo! Is someone there?" Her voice growing louder.

Joyce pressed her eye closer to the peephole, angling her body as though it would make her view through the peephole more visible.

"Maybe, it was my imagination," she said, questioning herself. "No! I heard footsteps," she said in a more confident tone. "There it is again," she whispered. The sound of footsteps stopped nearby her door.

Joyce gasped quietly. Her right eye opened so wide it appeared distorted, almost touching the glass cylinder peephole in the door. She stood on tippy-toes to raise her small frame and short stature to position herself for a better view.

"Hello," she screamed. "Oh, God...Why can't I just open the door?"

She touched the knob, her hands sticky and wet. Her heart started to race harder. Joyce spoke in a hushed tone to herself, "Just open the door...just open the door...step out to see what's out there."

Joyce could feel the irregular palpitation of her heart and beads of sweat developing on her brow. She jerked her hand quickly away from the knob. Her fear swelled between hot flashes and chills.

"No, don't...I can't, something's wrong! Don't open the door. Don't open the door."

Joyce strained to listen through the door. Her eyeball rigidly fixed on the hallway as she gazed intensely through the peephole.

"Why won't they answer? God, something is wrong. Someone is out there," she said softly.

"Go away! Go away and leave me alone!"

She started thinking about all the slasher movies she had seen. Her mind began to picture scenes of masked killers and strangulations.

"What if they try to get in here? A knife. Get a knife."

Joyce moved silently but hurriedly from the door, feeling her way through the darkness into the kitchen. Fumbling across the counter, she cut her finger on one of the knives in the knife holder on the kitchen counter.

"Ouch!" Joyce said, quickly drawing her finger to her lips to suck at the blood oozing from the small cut. She then reached carefully towards the holder and withdrew the largest of the butcher knives from it.

Back at the front door, she gazed through the peephole. There was a partially visible shadow to the left of the door. Her lip twitched for a second, her eye widened.

"What is that?" she asked, gripping the knife tightly.

Joyce strained to see the dimensional silhouette that seemed to grow right in front of her.

"Who's there?" she screamed again.

There was no answer. Suddenly, there was a loud blow, the sound of something thick and heavy striking the ground. Her heart began to beat violently as the striking noise began to resound again loudly.

Terrified, Joyce fell to the floor like a frightened child hiding from the view of the peephole. Cowering on her knees, she leaned, pressing her ear to the door, listening to the sound.

"Oh, my God...oh, my God," mumbling urgently under her breath. "Please protect me," she whispered.

Joyce thought about all the terrible things happening in the world, the awful things in the news.

They find victims my age all the time; her mind was racing. *Bodies buried in shallow graves, raped, murdered.*

Joyce began to visualize terrifying images of murdered women from the accumulation of violent late-night horror flicks she had watched over the years. While trying to force the horrifying images from her mind, she felt a sudden chill, becoming even more alarmed.

"Who is that?" she called out from the floor. "Phone. The phone. Call the police."

Joyce fumbled across the floor in the dark toward the direction of her phone. She grabbed the phone.

"Oh no... no! Damn! Damn!" The phone was not working.

"No electricity... no electricity," she said through garbled, low weeping.

Joyce thought about the many times Deacon Carter suggested she get a cell phone recalling her response.

What do I need a cell phone for when I have a perfectly working phone, just another unnecessary expense.

"Stupid," she muttered to herself.

Rising from the floor, Joyce felt her way back to the front door.

Pressing her body tightly against the door, Joyce situated her eye to the peephole. Her gaze remained fixed on the shadow. She could feel the thumping of her heartbeat as the indistinct image weaved across the wall from her doorway.

"Who are you? What do you want?"

Still no answer.

Joyce began to feel dizzy and nauseous. She wondered if she was going crazy.

"Maybe Deacon Carter was right. Maybe there is something wrong with me.

"Who is that?" she screamed hysterically.

It was approaching midnight. Joyce's glazed eye was still staring through the peephole. Her breathing was difficult and labored, and there was tingling along the left side of her body. Her heartbeat raced at a grueling pace. Her legs weakened from the strain of standing, while her level of fear heightened each time the shadowy image moved across the path of the peephole. Suddenly, an intense pain gushed through Joyce's entire body, flooding into her heart like a violent implosion. She gripped at her chest in paralyzing agony right before falling to the floor.

The next morning there was knocking at the door. It was Louie, the new building maintenance man.

Louie was a tiny, little man who stood just under three feet tall. Louie took great offense at being called a midget, preferring the term "little" rather than the host of labels that befell him, such as pygmy, leprechaun, or runt. He was also a deaf-mute, but he was one of the best electricians in town.

Louie worked on the electrical circuitry panel just outside of Joyce Carter's front door. He had run an electrical cord from a portable generator to a small lamp to illuminate the corridor while working through the night.

Louie lived in a world of complete silence from birth. As a small deaf child, he grew up seeing all the emotional and sometimes heinous results of constant chatter and inconsequential ranting all around him.

Coincidentally, Louie also enjoyed his life of silence, perfectly contented being outside the reach of the rest of the world. For him, the silent stillness of his surroundings was solitary, a godsend.

Knock, Knock, Knock.

Inside the apartment, Joyce lay at the base of the front door. Her eyes were frozen, with a far-off glassy stare. Terror marked her contorted and twisted face, still clutching at her now silenced heart. The butcher knife beside her. A slip of paper slid under the door, landing beside her stiffening body; it read:

The electrical problem has been corrected. Sorry for any inconvenience. From Louie, Maintenance.

9

THE HAT LADY

A light wind blew across the trees outside the large picture window as Ms. Agatha Canterbury's eyes scanned the empty living room. Her soft wrinkled skin quickly revealed her age; she had recently turned seventy-two. A pleasing smile graced her face as she recalled the memories of the past year in her home. Beside her, an open hat box rested on top of two large stacked cardboard boxes.

She lifts a raisin colored velvet boater hat with a satin flower and sizeable black feather accent from the box. Strokes it like a sweet child, then places it on her head.

Zeus, a white Siamese cat, struts aloof across the room.

"Well... my dear Zeus, it is that time again. Time for us to move on," she said, her smile growing more significant.

Zeus bolts in the opposite direction as a man hurriedly enters through the open front door wearing a bay breeze mesh hat. Pushing a hand dolly in front of him, he snaps up the two large boxes with the hatbox atop and heads back outside.

"These are the last boxes. The neighborhood won't be the same without you, Ms. Canterbury," he said as he headed out the door.

"I'm sure we will one day meet again," she replies over a short chuckle as she smiles across the room in Zeus' direction.

"Come... come to me, Zeus. It's time to go."

Two days later, and miles away, the morning sun etches across the porch where a For Rent sign rests beside a rocking chair near the door. The front screen door whips open. A burly man lurches out in a tee-shirt stained with sweat. Wiping his brow with a dirty rag, he moves briskly down the porch steps. A second man follows with Ms. Canterbury right behind him. She stops in the doorway. He stops short of her, his face wet with sweat as he turns to Ms. Canterbury.

"That's everything, ma'am. I just need you to sign the paperwork." He extends a clipboard at her. She signs.

As Ms. Canterbury hands the clipboard with the signed paperwork back over to him, she glances across the street. Fingers emerged between closed window blinds creating a small opening. Ms. Canterbury could not see the eyes peering through, just the slight movement. She turns her attention to the moving truck as it pulls away from her new residence. Her eyes follow it as it travels down the street, disappearing around the corner.

Turning back towards the window across the street, she waves. The blinds quickly close shut. Ms. Canterbury chuckles as she turns and enters her home.

The following morning, Ms. Canterbury maneuvers down the steps carrying an A-frame sign as Zeus sits on the windowsill inside the living room, peering out. His eyes follow her every move. She places the sign on the lawn and paces back a few steps to glance down at it with an approving nod. The sign reads THE HAT LADY.

From behind the comfort of her living room picture window, Ms. Canterbury looks out across the somber neighborhood lined with weather-worn homes and unkempt lawns. Two houses down, Paul Williams, a tall, handsomely suited man in his late 30s, storms angrily out. Samantha Williams, a youthfully attracted woman, follows behind in tears.

"What do you want me to do?" she cries as Paul jumps in a car and speeds off. Samantha yells in the direction of the vehicle.

"Paul, we need to figure this out together!"

Farther down the street, ten-year-old Johnny Johnson pushes another kid to the ground. Ms. Canterbury watches as the kid jumps up and takes off running. Johnny chases after him. She shakes her head disapprovingly.

Ms. Canterbury's eyes drift back across the street, observing the small opening in the window blinds before it quickly swings shut. A slow, deliberate smile appears on Ms. Canterbury's face.

Several days later, across the street, Birdie Hughes presses her fingers against the blinds, she peeks through the small slit. Her body sways slightly as one hand clutches a walking cane. She is seventy-five, and her wrinkled face and stark gray hair is a telling sign of her age. Her husband, Henry Hughes, sits on the couch. The sound is low on the old black and white movie on the TV screen. A half-eaten sandwich sits on the coffee table in front of him. Dusk is about to fall, yet still light enough for Birdie to spy on her new neighbor.

"Henry. Henry, something's going on over there."

"Uh-huh," said Henry, staring into the TV. Birdie frowns in Henry's direction, seeing he is paying her no attention.

"Henry! Did you hear what I said? I'm telling you something's not right."

Henry shrugged, "Birdie, she's selling hats, what's wrong with that?"

Birdie continues to peer through the blinds. Her voice is monotonous and low.

"No, Henry, something just doesn't feel right. That old cantankerous Mr. Simmons was there yesterday, and Mrs. Connelly, that snobby woman, walked out of her house last Friday."

Henry sighed loudly and looked over at Birdie with a serious frankness.

"Birdie, were they wearing hats?"

"Yes, Henry, they were wearing hats."

"I rest my case!"

"But no one wears hats like these anymore," she whispers to herself. Turning to Henry, "That brat Johnny Johnson came out of her house this morning wearing an ascot cap. Kids don't wear ascot caps these days."

"Birdie, what do you want me to tell you? You spend too much time in that window."

"That trouble-making kid needs a switch to his bottom... not a new hat. Something is going on over there, Henry. Something is going on."

Henry says nothing as he continues to stare at the TV. Birdie continues to peer quietly through the small opening in the blinds.

A month has passed on the sleepy little street. There is the distant sound of a door opening, and a German Shepard darts out of the house a few doors down across the street from Ms. Canterbury. The dog runs right over to the neighboring yard, sniffs around, and turns in circles. Just as the dog starts to squat, George Briggs charges out of his front door. He yells, chasing after the startled German Shepard as it runs off.

"Go crap in your own yard. Keep your dog off my property," he yells while giving the middle finger towards the direction of his neighbor's house.

Ms. Canterbury caresses Zeus watching from the rocking

chair on her front porch. Zeus hisses as the German Shepard runs past, seeking another yard to squat in.

That afternoon, inside Ms. Canterbury's home, a collection of hats displayed on mannequin heads are situated throughout the room. A woman wearing a pair of ill-fitted rimmed glasses tries on a cocktail hat with red silk rose curls and an organza bow. She smiles broadly at herself in a mirror. Later, a middle-aged man exits her home wearing a stylish, felt fedora hat.

As the evening sun begins to set, Ms. Canterbury rocks back and forth in the front porch chair. Zeus curled beside her. Suddenly loud voices from a few houses down are heard. Ms. Canterbury and Zeus turn simultaneously towards the sound.

Paul Williams rushes angrily from the house. A tearful Samantha follows. Catching him, she grabs his arm.

"This is our problem, not just mines. I'm trying Paul."

"This is not what I signed up for, Samantha." snapped Paul.

"It's not my fault I can't get pregnant. Maybe it's not me. Maybe it's an issue with you."

"Don't point the finger at me. You know I've always wanted a son."

"And I've been trying to give you a son for six years now."

Paul jerks away from Samantha's hold on his arm.

"Try harder."

Samantha's lips quiver and she begins to cry as Paul jumps into his car, revs the engine, and drives off. Samantha angrily paces down the street towards the direction of Ms. Canterbury's house. As Samantha tearfully nears, Ms. Canterbury calls out to her.

"Dear, dear... Come here a moment, please, please come along. I bet we could both use a hot cup of tea right about now."

Inside, Ms. Canterbury reaches for the tea kettle on the coffee table in front of her. She pours tea into two cups. Samantha's eyes red from crying takes a sip.

"I'm Samantha Williams. How kind of you, you didn't have to."

"Of course, I did. It's nice to have someone to talk to besides my hats," Ms. Canterbury said with a giggle.

Samantha chuckles through sobs. She glances around the room.

"Your hats are exquisite; do you make them all yourself?"

"These hands have made many hats over the years."

Samantha takes a large gulp of tea. "I'm sorry you had to see my husband Paul and me behaving this way. He is a good man."

"I'm sure he is dear...I'm sure he is."

"He's just... well, he's unhappy," said Samantha. "He's always wanted a son. It's put so much pressure on our marriage."

Samantha begins to cry softly. "I just can't seem to give him one."

Ms. Canterbury hands her a napkin. Samantha dabs her eyes and nose.

"This will pass, you'll see. You come back tomorrow. I have a hat in mind for you."

"Oh no, I can't afford to pay for one of your hats."

"It's a gift, dear. You won't deny an old lady some pleasure now, would you?

A small smile slid over Samantha's face.

The sun had gone down, making way for the delicate moonlight that spilled through the workroom window. Ms. Canterbury sat in a cluttered room filled with several large bins of fabrics and hat frames. The many shelves lining the walls contained materials, scissors, tools, ribbons, and bows. With mannequin heads topped with finished and unfinished hats, some appearing centuries old, others bare.

Ms. Canterbury sat at a large worktable, threading a ribbon in place on a wool derby bowler hat. Two large candles sat on each side of the hat. Gentle smoke billows up from incense in an antique carved incense holder. The smell of musk filled the air, an incense burned for heightening sensual passions.

As the night continued to enter through the corner of a window shade falling uneven along the windowsill, the light from a single lamp spills across Ms. Canterbury's face as time passes further into the night.

The hat, now exquisitely adorned with ribbons, lace, and bows, sat on the table in front of her. Zeus nestled under the table at her feet. The sound of the clock chimes quietly twelve times. It is now midnight, and Ms. Canterbury smiles favorably at her results.

The following day the front door of Ms. Canterbury's house swings opens. Samantha walks out wearing an eloquently finished Derby bowler hat. A large white feather protrudes from the band—Ms. Canterbury waves after Samantha.

Seconds later, a police car pulls up in front of Ms. Canterbury's house. An officer exits the vehicle and walks towards her.

"Hello, I'm officer Arden. We received a complaint, ma'am, about the amount of traffic and people coming in and out of your house." Looking at the sign in her yard, he continues. "I see you are doing business from your home. Do you know that this area is not zoned for business?"

"Well, it's more of a hobby officer, but I do have some paperwork I can show you. Please come in for a moment, maybe a cup of tea for you as well?"

Ms. Canterbury glances across the street to the cracked window blinds, which immediately spring shut. The officer follows her inside. An hour later, the officer exits Ms. Canterbury's front door, smiling broadly. An oilcloth trapper hat on his head.

Across the street, two older women are now standing on Birdie's front porch. Henrietta Burns, a thinly petite woman, and Mrs. Doris Jones, a well-fed, sharply dressed woman. They watch as the officer enters his car. Opening the door, Birdie peaks her head out, as they all three turn in unison towards Ms. Canterbury's direction. Ms. Canterbury waves.

Without acknowledging, they enter Birdie's home. Ms. Canterbury lets out a low throaty laugh.

Inside Birdie's house, Henry is seated on his regular end of the couch. The TV plays quietly in the background. The ladies fill the two available seats on the sofa next to him. Birdie flops down into the armchair beside the couch, placing her walking cane beside her.

"The police just don't do their jobs! She is doing business on our block, and he buys a hat. I'm telling you; something is not right!" Birdie said sarcastically.

"Well, she must have a permit to do business; otherwise, the officer wouldn't have bought a hat from her," said Doris.

Glancing at Birdie, Henrietta remarked, "Her hats must be nice. She seems to be selling quite a few of them. Everybody seems to be buying them."

Chiming in, Henry cynically replies, "Do you think maybe people just like hats?"

"I'm telling you, there's something more going on over there," snapped Birdie.

Henry let out a deep grunt.

"Did you see the hat Mrs. Albright had on the other day?" asked Doris. "To be honest, I wouldn't mind having one."

"This isn't funny, Doris! I'm telling you something's not right," replied an annoyed Birdie.

"Well, why doesn't someone just go over there and check it out?" asked Henrietta. They all turn simultaneously towards Henry.

"Don't look at me. I'm not in this," said Henry.

"The hats are elaborate. But I'm not sure why anyone wants to walk around in feathers and bows these days?" said Henrietta.

"I like feathers and bows," chimed Doris.

"Doris, you starting to get on my last nerve," said an annoyed Birdie. Under her breath, Doris replied, "Well, I do."

"Henry, go check it out," Birdie demanded in a harsh tone.

"You're kidding. Birdie, I don't want to go bothering that woman."

"Let me put it this way, Henry, this is not a request," Birdie replied angrily.

Doris and Henrietta glance at one another through soft giggles. Doris whispers to Henrietta, "Somebody got up on the wrong side of the bed this morning."

Henrietta whispers in response to Doris, "She gets up on the wrong side of the bed every morning." They both continue to giggle—Henry grunts in frustration.

There was a slight chill in the afternoon air as a dapper middle-aged man exits Ms. Canterbury's front door wearing a derby bowler black hat.

That evening, a pretty young woman touches up her lipstick. She wears a fancy garden party hat with a substantial floral laced bow and satin ribbon. She admires herself in a large hand mirror as Ms. Canterbury looks on.

"I simply love it. Thank you so much, Ms. Canterbury," the woman gleamed as she rose from her seat.

The doorbell rings as they approach the door. It's Henry Hughes.

"Thank you. Goodbye, dear." Ms. Canterbury directed her attention to her new visitor, "Well, good evening Mr. Hughes, come on in."

Henry responds in surprise, "You know who I am?"

"Of course, I do, dear; this is a small community, now isn't it." Henry enters Ms. Canterbury's home. The door closes shut behind him.

Awakening from a deep sleep, Birdie struggles to her feet with the help of the walking stick beside her bed. She enters the living room. The room is dark except for static light from the TV.

Henry lay slumped, dead asleep on the couch. A lambskin ascot cap on his head. He lets out a quiet groan and mild snore.

"Useless old fool. Send you out, and you come back with a stupid hat on your head."

Birdie walks over to the front window. The sound of her walking stick taps the floor. She peeks through the blinds. Turning towards Henry, now snoring loudly, she wears a distressed look of concern on her face.

Ms. Canterbury sits at her worktable. A collection of ancient religious images line the fireplace mantel. The sky is unusually dark this night, as though the moon had drifted asleep overhead.

Before her, dim shafts of light fall on a hat nestled between two lit candles and small statues of Greek Hellenist gods. The smell of Patchouli oil diffused throughout the air. Zeus nestled beside her feet. She lifts the hat.

"Hideaway, the fear of the wearer, remove all anxiety, the hat holds power to control."

Zeus stares towards the wall; he hears the distant sound of light tapping along the pathway on the side of the house.

"Hideaway, the fear of the wearer, remove all anxiety, the hat holds power to control." Ms. Canterbury lifts an incense wand, waving it as smoke wafts through the air.

The tapping now closer. Zeus quickly sits upright at movement beyond the window.

Birdie peaks through a narrow opening in the window shade as Zeus let out a hiss at her presence. The clock on the mantel chimes twelve times, announcing midnight.

Ms. Canterbury rises to her feet. Her eyes close, she spreads her hands full as the sound of the table rumbling rises.

"I call upon my fallen angels. Assa, Enepsigos, Lillith, Orobas, we build together with our army of lost souls."

An immense shadow looms across the wall. Two broad black wings spread wide from Ms. Canterbury's silhouette.

Birdie freezes, her eyes widen to a look of dread as a soul-shattering chill befalls her. The sound of soft repetitive uttered whispers fills the room.

"Darkness within. Lost souls between worlds. Soothe your woes, Enepsigos, possession, Assa, Orobas, temptation," the whispers quietly chant in the background.

"Hats hold power," Ms. Canterbury continues. "Hats hold the power. Transport the wearer, conceal the suffering oh powerful one."

"Capture their souls, capture their souls," the background whispers continue.

"Power in the hats, souls of the damned, exposed, hidden illusions, spirits of nature," bellows Ms. Canterbury.

"The darkness within, whence we came, in our darkest night, we recall, lost sufferers, Lillith." The sound of whispers surge throughout the room.

Zeus' eyes suddenly locked onto Birdies. The cat stands with his back arched high, his white fur morphs to black. Zeus let's out a loud hissing shrill.

Ms. Canterbury whirls around, her face stunningly youthful, her eyes frighteningly evil, glow reddish-yellow. She stares at Birdie, who is now frozen with fear.

The now looming shadow plucks a black feather from one of its wings. The room's illuminance glows red like the brightness of a bloodied sun. Birdie lets out a loud piercing scream as she stumbles back in horror. The room falls silent.

While summer passes into fall, fall passes into spring, brown and orange fall leaves surround and blow past the yard sign on Ms. Canterbury's front lawn. The sign withered from hard rain over the passing nightfall's and daylight risings time and time again. Over the months, a cast of characters come and go from Ms. Canterbury's house.

Doris and Henrietta both radiate with excitement as they

leave wearing twin vintage big bowed pillbox hats.

George Shepard nods pleasingly as he looks up from a mirror clutched in his hand. He wears a wool felt trilby hat on his head. Zeus, glowing in his immaculate white furry coat, curls on the couch beside him.

It was hotter this summer than it had ever been over the past ten months as Ms. Canterbury panned the neighborhood through her living room window. Zeus in her arms.

"Our work is almost done here, Zeus...soon our army of followers will be everywhere. And from the wound, he shall come to lead."

She glances a few houses down at Samantha, who kisses Paul as he leaves for work. Her pregnant belly is amply visible, her baby due any day now. A grimacing smile stretches across Ms. Canterbury's face.

"Soon, my master's son arrives. Soon."

A few houses down, a man pushes a lawnmower. Nearby a woman waters her lawn. A German Shepard runs over to George Briggs; he pats the dog on the head. Lively neighbors spill out of their homes.

Children frolic. People happily greet one another. Johnny Johnson tosses newspapers on lawns as he rides his bike down the street. Everyone is wearing one of Ms. Canterbury's hats.

Across the street, the blinds raised, the front window view wide open. Birdie stands without her walking stick as she waves in Ms. Canterbury's direction. A beautiful ivy Panama cloche hat on her head.

10

DANGEROUS MAN

"Oh, my goodness, tell us about this little guy," said Jane Schaffer, host of 'Today's Events' daily talk show.

"This is Ace, and he is a bearded dragon. They originated from Australia and can grow to up to two feet long. And, surprisingly, they make great house pets, and they are also good with children."

"So, what inspired you to rescue exotic pets," asked Schaffer.

"Well, I've been an animal lover all my life. My first rescue was an Ostrich that had been left behind by its owner when he lost his property to foreclosure."

"Wow," responded Jane.

"Yeah, it was a little hairy at first because they can be really mean. You don't want to get kicked by an Ostrich.

However, it came around, and I think it thought it was just another one of my dogs. I called him 'Feathers,' he has since been placed with an Ostrich Rescue Farm in Solvang, California."

"Well, I think what you do is wonderful, and I am amazed that you find the time to do all these remarkable things. You are one of the most popular celebrities in the world. You're working on your next feature film. You contribute to the community; you work with youth. Okay, audience, let's give Milo Mason a big round of applause."

As the audience applauds loudly, Josh Harrison stares into the television screen. Josh admired Milo Mason; he was Josh's favorite actor. Josh began following Milo's acting career as a teen. He loved the high energy suspenseful movies in which Milo Mason was most celebrated.

Josh, an inspiring actor, moved to Los Angeles when he was twenty-one. Now twenty-nine, he has pursued his career in Hollywood for eight years, with less than enthusiastic success. Josh took jobs washing dishes and cleaning up cages at veterinary offices. He attended casting calls when he could, securing several small roles in a few major films and some minor parts in others. However, his favorite extra part was on the set of a movie featuring Milo Mason. It was one of the best experiences of his life. Josh didn't get the opportunity to speak to Milo, but his character stood nearby him as one of the background actors on the set.

Milo Mason, a handsome man of thirty-eight, could easily be mistaken for someone closer to Josh's age. He was physically fit and maintained a pretty boy appearance that all of Hollywood and the world loved. Milo starred in some of the best movie's Josh had ever seen.

Later that evening, Josh watched one of Milo Mason's earlier movies, one he had seen about six times before. As he viewed it, it was as though he was in the film, right there with Milo.

"Get him! Don't let him get away!" Jason screamed at the TV screen.

"Look behind you! He's right behind you! Shoot the mother fucka!"

Josh felt exhilarated after the movie. He released a loud burp as he pulled the tab on his fifth can of beer, swigging it as though he had personally apprehended the villain.

Josh made it a point to show up at every movie and premier opening for Milo Mason that he could attend. He watched his interviews and participated in all of Milo's public events. Josh was one of his best fans. So much so, he started a Fan of Milo Mason page on a social media platform where he boasted about his over 1.3 million followers.

Josh would spend hours in front of the mirror, mimicking Milo's voice and movements. He wanted to be like Milo Mason and was becoming more obsessed with him every day. Josh studied everything about Milo. He knew where he was born, where he grew up. He knew he was single with no family, a generous philanthropist, and where he lived.

Josh's obsessions grew more intense over the next year. He began to follow Milo's movements, including driving past his vast 25 million-dollar, 30,000 square foot villa located on seven acres in the Hollywood Hills. Josh coveted Milo's life and became more curious about the world behind the elaborate wrought-iron gate surrounding Milo Mason's home.

Josh was drained from the long shift as the restaurant busboy brought the last pile of dirty dishes to the kitchen. As he removed the soaking pots and pans and loaded them into the commercial dishwasher, the small mounted TV set in the kitchen made the time pass easier. He perked up, hearing the name Milo Mason in the background, and turned to glance up at the TV screen. Milo was responding to a question.

"My new film, 'Dangerous Man,' will begin filming tomorrow. The production will mean long, exhaustive days. Still, I'm thrilled to be working with James Compton, the film's director, once again," said Milo.

A large macaw parrot sat perched on a wooden branch in an enormous cage. Its beautiful cobalt-blue plumage and dark yellow-ringed eyes perked up at the distant sound of breaking glass.

Light footsteps paced the floor as Josh Harrison tiptoed through the rear laundry room into an immaculate, spacious kitchen in Milo Mason's home. Josh carried a plastic bag with pieces of raw meat injected with a sedation drug he stole from one of the veterinary offices. Tossing the chunky morsels at the dogs roaming the exterior grounds, they quickly gobbled up the edibles as Josh rushed toward the house. He held on to the remaining pieces in case any of the dogs were inside the home; he knew the tainted meat would sedate the dogs for a few hours.

Milo's new movie was filming today, so this was Josh's opportunity to finally see the inside of Milo's home. As Josh moved through the house, his eyes widened at the high ceilings and size of the rooms. After entering the grand entry, he was startled by a macaw, who immediately began to squawk and flap its wings.

"Hello. Hello, Hello," mimicked the macaw peering from the cage housed in the main foyer area to welcome house guests. Josh hid for a moment, listening for movement. Two pot-belly pigs ran playfully across the foyer and into the nearby study. Josh chuckled at the sight of them and continued to move through the home quietly.

There was a mini-movie theater, a lavish game room with a full sports bar. The large spa-like bathrooms included huge shower jets with separate sauna tubs. Josh began to sprint through the house a bit faster, comfortable that no one was there. He quickly hurried up the two-story staircase, entering the second level of the home. There were so many bedrooms, but he came across what he felt was Milo's room. It was a beautiful, ample, luxuriously furnished space that looked across a backyard. The area included a large swimming pool, spa, cabana, built-in food preparation station, a stunning stone patio with outdoor furnishings, and a nearby waterfall. Milo felt a moment of being in heaven; it was striking, the life he always wanted. He felt even more inspired to become a successful actor.

The bearded dragon Josh watched in an interview with Milo a year earlier was much bigger now. It rested on a large chaise lounge chair in the corner of the room.

Josh entered the massive walk-in closet. His eyes widened as he stared across the line of shirts and slacks hanging on racks. Josh opened drawers containing rows of watches, rings, and cuff links. He picked up one of the rings and slid it on his finger.

The abrupt sound of electric rolling shutters shocked Josh. He rushed from the closet in time to see the windows being sealed off from the outside by security shutters slowly moving down over the windows. Josh quickly darted out of the room and bounded down the stairs to the foyer. By the time Josh reached the front door, the double-bolt security locks were already activated, and the shutters covered the exterior door and foyer windows. The external room light vanished from the now sealed home. Josh Harrison panicked.

A voice came over the intercom.

"You do know it's against the law to trespass into a man's home, don't you?"

Josh recognized the voice as Milo Mason.

"I'm sorry! I didn't mean anything."

"I'm not," replied Milo.

Josh's nostrils flared as his breathing became rapid inhalations. He frantically dashed through the house, passing sealed windows heading back through the kitchen and towards the laundry room, hoping that he might make it out where he came in. The laundry room window and the door were both sealed shut.

"Too late, too late, too late for you," Milo teased, in a lusty song-like tone.

As Josh reentered the kitchen, he glanced towards the door to the dining area to see a red fox standing in the doorway staring at him. Jessie quickly grabbed an apple sitting in a bowl of fruit on the island counter and threw it in the direction of the red wolf. The wolf let out a short high-pitched shrill as it immediately darted away.

"Aw, now that wasn't nice," said Milo.

"Look, I said I'm sorry. I just wanted to see your home. I thought you would be on set. I just wanted to see... please, I'm not here to steal anything from you."

"Oh, really. Isn't that my ring on your finger?"

"I wasn't going to keep it. I was going to put it back!"

"Of course, you were."

"Please, please let me out. I just wanted to see how you live!"

"I know, I often have fans like you drop by," said Milo snidely, continuing. "I call them stalkers."

"I'm not a stalker. I'm just a fan!" Cried Josh, sorrowfully. "I would never threaten or hurt you."

"Oh, yes, you are. You're a naughty little stalker." Milo's voice bellowed over the intercom.

Josh's legs were sporadically shaking as he bolted again, running scared through the house.

The macaw's wings flapped as it squawked louder and louder.

"Hello. Hello. Hello. Run! Run! Run!" mimicked the macaw repeatedly.

Josh terrified, still racing frantically through the house, looking for an escape. He found himself back near the kitchen near a door slightly cracked open. Josh grabbed the knob and flung the door wide open. Stairs appeared to lead down towards a basement. Thinking he might be able to find an escape in the basement, he sprinted down the stairs.

Once reaching the bottom, he lunged ahead, hurriedly scrambling around stacked boxes, covered furnishings, and massive statuettes, hoping for a window, a way to escape. There were no windows, but there was a door. He darted towards it, jerking it open and rushing through. It was a wine cellar with rows and rows of bottles. Dropping the bag of tainted meat, he grabbed a bottle of wine and smashed it. Both shards of glass and wine flew in all directions, spilling across the floor. Josh clutched the bottle's neck tightly in his hand; the sharp broken end pointed ahead of him.

Milo's laughter loomed throughout the house as though readying to banish a child to stand in a corner.

"Tsk, tsk, tsk," Milo said mockingly. "That was a bottle of Chateau Lafite 1787. A one hundred fifty-six-thousand-dollar bottle of wine, young man. What a waste!"

Josh rushed hysterically through the wine cellar, spotting another door ahead. He darted towards the door, opened it, and ran in. After Josh entered the dimly lit room, the door slammed shut behind him. Then the sound of an automatic latch closing. He immediately tried to reopen the door but could not. A terror-stricken Josh turned and stepped further into the lowly lite, soundproof underground conclave.

Suddenly, a sound more frightening than anything Josh had ever heard deafens him. It was the roar of a 490-pound Bengal Tiger. The tiger stared at him from a large gated zoo-like compound containing an indoor tropical habitat stretching over 3 miles beneath the home.

Milo's voice blasted overhead.

"Meet Danger. Isn't he magnificent? He loves visitors, especially at dinner time."

The electronically gated doors of the enclosure slowly began to open, and Danger slowly approached his prey.

Three weeks later, Milo added the newspaper headline clipping to his trophy wall, which read *Social Media Followers Are Asking 'What Happened to Josh Harrison?' Hopes of Finding Him Alive Dwindle*. Milo stepped back to admire dozens of newspaper clippings, the missing faces of his obsessed fans.

The following day Milo was on the production set of his new film 'Dangerous Man.' The production had been going well. The combat scene between Milo's character and his villainous co-star playing his childhood friend, now on the wrong side of the law, was just wrapping up.

"I'm sorry we were like brothers. I didn't mean for this to happen," said the antagonist.

Milo pulls a gun from his vest holster and points it at his head. He shoots.

"Cut," calls the Director. "This scene is just not working. We need something more."

"Why don't you give my character a short line after he says he's sorry? Something like, I'm not!" said Milo.

"Great idea Milo." The Director continued, "Let's try it again with that line added. Milo, you come up with some great stuff. Roll sound. Roll camera!"

The Second Assistant Camera slates with a clapperboard and calls out the scene, "Scene 16, Take 9."

"Action!"

11

BERNADETTE

Bernadette filled the washer with a second load before folding and arranging her freshly dried towels into two tidy bundles. It was nearing early evening, and the entire day had been perfect as usual. As she double-checked the washer's temperature setting, she caught sight of her image in the mirror hanging against the laundry room wall. You would have never guessed from her appearance how busy she'd been all day—cleaning the house, caring for the children, making homemade play dough, and putting the finishing touches on dinner.

Bernadette's appearance was immaculate, her hair perfectly arranged, and she was always neatly attired. Today she wore her favorite powder-blue skirt with tiny floral print and a white cotton blouse that appeared incredibly crisp.

As a child, Bernadette always dreamed of having the perfect family when she got older. Unlike the family she grew up with, where both her mother and father were abusive alcoholics

Those were miserable days for Bernadette, but things were so much different now. She finally had the home and family she always dreamed about, the family she always wanted.

Her family gave her life, and she enjoyed every moment of the day that she could simply please them. She worked hard to provide them the ideal environment and to maintain her perfect appearance.

Bernadette was not an unattractive woman, but there was nothing notably beautiful about her, either. She was a tall, thin woman with long legs and awkwardly broad shoulders. Her butter-cream complexion was crowded with sprinklings of brown freckles, complimenting her honey-brown hair.

Chelsea called out from the kitchen, and Bernadette instantly switched her attention to her daughter's voice.

"Look, mommy! Look! I made a piggy," she gleamed in high pitch from the adjoining room. Chelsea was an utterly adorable seven-year-old with pinchable, rosy cheeks. Her face drizzled in freckles like her mother's, a compliment to her naturally pink lips. Her thick blond hair twisted in dozens of curly tufts.

"That is wonderful, darling. I'll be right there. Mommy wants to see your little piggy."

"I made a happy face, mommy," said little Jimmy, Jr., wanting the same accolade.

"Ooooh, Jimmy. I can't wait to see your happy face, too!" Bernadette turned and smiled at her reflection in the mirror.

Everything was perfect, she thought to herself, and she childishly licked her tongue at her image before leaving the laundry room.

Bernadette walked over to the breakfast nook where both Chelsea and Jimmy, Jr. sat. An array of colorful play dough rounds and craft magnets lay before them.

"They're wonderful," she squealed as she slid into the seat beside Jimmy, Jr. "Did you make these? You couldn't have made these!"

Jimmy nodded vigorously. "Yes, I did, mommy. I made them all by myself." His broad smile nearly covered his chubby little face. He was the younger of the two, five years old, and what a perfect little boy he was! Bernadette never experienced the dreaded terrible two's or three's with either of them. They both were wonderfully behaved children.

"But they're so good. How did you learn to make such pretty magnets?"

"I don't know," said Jimmy appreciatively.

"Me neither," chimed Chelsea.

"But surely, you must have gone to college for this or had some special magical training."

"That's silly, mommy, we're not old enough to go to college," giggled Chelsea.

"Yeah, mommy!" Jimmy exploded with laughter.

"Well, they're just wonderful."

"What's wonderful?" asked Jim as he entered the room. Jim walked over to the trio and leaned over, kissing Bernadette quickly on the lips.

"Look, honey," Bernadette said, "Look at the lovely magnets. Aren't they simply wonderful?"

"They sure are! Chelsea, where did you and Jimmy buy your magnets?" Jim asked.

"We didn't buy them, daddy! We made them!" said Chelsea giggling.

"Wow. Isn't that something," Jim said with a burst of laughter.

"Dinner will be ready soon, honey. We're having your favorite, roast beef and mashed potatoes."

"Smells wonderful, honey. You're the best cook in town."

"Why don't you go into the living room, honey? Put your feet up and watch the evening news until dinner. I'll bring you a glass of iced tea."

Bernadette never served leftovers. When she was little, she used to eat leftovers day in and day out—sometimes reaching way back into the refrigerator to find two-or three-week-old scraps or eat nothing at all. She swore she would never serve day-old meals to her family. Jim and the kids deserved better than that, and Bernadette made sure that they received three freshly prepared meals daily.

"Okay, honey, um um... I can hardly wait!" said Jim as he leaned over and gave Bernadette another peck on the lips.

"I'll make a magnet, especially for you, daddy," bubbled Chelsea, as Jim walked toward the living room.

"Me too, daddy," mimicked Jimmy, Jr.

Jim was a wonderful husband, a great provider, and a great father. Bernadette could not have wished for a better marriage. Everything about Jim was perfect.

Bernadette leaned over and hugged Jimmy.

"Start clearing the table off. Dinner will be ready soon, and I want you both to go wash up and get ready."

"Okay, mommy." They both replied in unison.

Bernadette walked over to the oven and lowered the temperature on the roast.

"Should be ready in a few," she said under her breath. As she began to stir the potatoes simmering on the stove, the doorbell rang.

"Honey, will you get the door?" she yelled at Jim. DING-DONG. DING-DONG.

"Chelsea, go tell your daddy to get the door." Bernadette turned to look towards the breakfast nook. The area was empty.

"Well, what do you know, there's a first time for everything," she thought. The table was clear, and the kids had already gone upstairs to wash up. DING DONG! DING DONG! DING DONG!

"Jim... Jim!" Bernadette called. DING DONG!

"Just a minute!" she shouted, "I'll be right there!"

Bernadette turned the potatoes off and hurried to the front door. She glanced over to the couch as she entered the living room. The TV was still on.

"No wonder our electricity is so high. Jim never remembers to turn off the TV," she mumbled to herself as she grabbed hold of the knob handle and quickly pulled the door open.

"Hello, Bernadette."

"Dr. Walsh," Bernadette said in a startled tone, "What are you doing here?"

"I've missed seeing you, Bernadette. You missed your last four appointments with me."

"I've been busy, Dr. Walsh," Bernadette said pointedly.

"But you haven't returned any of my calls."

"Well... I'm busy with housework right now, and I'm right in the middle of dinner. Jim and the kids are probably starving about now."

"I won't take up much of your time, Bernadette," said Dr. Walsh as she aggressively stepped inside, forcing Bernadette to take a step back.

Bernadette hesitated momentarily before closing the door and trailing behind Dr. Walsh, who had already headed toward the dining room.

"You know how important it is for you to come to your sessions, Bernadette. Have you been taking your medications?" Dr. Walsh stopped at the end of the dining table and turned to Bernadette, anticipating her response.

"Ah...actually...I'm so much better, Dr. Walsh... I mean, everything is simply perfect in my life right now. I'm feeling better than ever, and I don't think I need to see you anymore."

Dr. Walsh turned away from Bernadette and began to stroll around the dining table, looking down at the perfectly displayed table settings for four. There was an attractive bouquet of fresh flowers in the center and lighted candles that matched the perfectly crisp table linen.

"Smells good, Bernadette, expecting company?" said Dr. Walsh.

Bernadette was dumbfounded by her question.

"No," she responded curiously. "Just, Jim... Jim and the children," she said, shifting her eyes away from Dr. Walsh and looking down towards the floor.

Dr. Walsh walked up to Bernadette and moved to grasp her hands.

"Bernadette! Look at me!" Demanded Dr. Walsh, failing to take Bernadette's hands into hers as she jerked them away in a frightened, yet defensive, manner.

Dr. Walsh continued, "Bernadette, do you remember why you were coming to see me?"

"I can't talk about this now, Dr. Walsh," said Bernadette, scowling. "I have to get dinner ready!"

"We have to talk about it, Bernadette. We've been over this, many times before!"

"I won't listen to you, doctor!" Bernadette's voice swelled with anger.

"Remember when you were a little girl, Bernadette. Your parents were very insensitive to you. They mistreated you and hurt you badly. Do you remember, Bernadette?"

Bernadette did not want to hear Dr. Walsh. She wrinkled

her face, distastefully like a little child as Dr. Walsh continued.

"Try to remember our discussions, Bernadette. Remember how you always dreamed of the perfect family? You always said that when you grew up, you would have the perfect family, the best family in the whole wide world. Remember, Bernadette, think! You became obsessed, Bernadette. You grew up hating your parents so much that you created your own perfect family."

Bernadette began to tremble as hot tears filled her eyes.

"Your imaginary family became so important to you, so real, so believable that you thought they could replace your real family. You wanted to replace your parents. Think Bernadette, think! You thought that if you could get rid of your parents, your imaginary family would be able to take over."

"Stop it, Dr. Walsh! Stop it, please! I don't want to hear any more of this! I must get dinner ready. I have to get dinner for Jim and my children!"

"Please, Bernadette! I need you to focus, and I need you to think. Remember the fire, Bernadette? Remember the night you set fire to your parents' bed? You were only seven years old. The same age as your imaginary Chelsea is now. Your parents were drunks. They drank, and they beat you. That night, while they slept, you set fire to their bed. Your parents died that night, Bernadette!"

"Stop this! Stop it now!" cried Bernadette. "It's not true! I must ask you to leave now, doctor!"

"That was twenty years ago, Bernadette. For the past

twenty years, you were confined to the state institute for the mentally insane. You were released only three months ago as part of a test program to see if you could adjust to the outside world. This home is a part of the program to see if you can manage alone. However, the program requires you to continue your treatment with me."

"No... no, it's not true," Bernadette said as the tears rolled down her cheeks.

"Bernadette, this is a court-ordered treatment. If you do not continue your sessions with me, I will have to report you. I will send you back to the institution. Do you understand me? Do you understand what is happening here, Bernadette? I will be forced to send you back to the asylum."

"It's a lie!" shouted Bernadette as her heart raced in sickening thumps.

"There is no Jim! There is no Chelsea. There is no Jimmy, Jr.! You made them up, Bernadette!" Dr. Walsh continued her voice stern and raised.

"They are all a part of your imagination! They're all a part of your perfect family, your dream."

"Liar! Liar!" Bernadette's body trembled as she screamed. Dr. Walsh sensed Bernadette's complete loss of control and attempted to retake her hands to calm her. Bernadette abruptly reached past Dr. Walsh and picked up a large carving knife lying on the table.

"Liar!" screamed Bernadette as she thrust the blade into Dr. Walsh's chest. Dr. Walsh let out a forced gasping sob.

"It's a lie! Liar! Liar!" Bernadette plunged the blade

deeper into her chest.

It happened so quickly. You could barely see the tears stream down Dr. Walsh's face or hear her waning murmur as the blood gurgled from her mouth. She slumped to the floor. When her body hit the ground, Bernadette dropped the carving knife and ran from the dining room.

Her petrifying screams echoed as she raced through the house. "Jim! Jim! Where are you!... Chelsea! Chelsea! Jimmy!" she shouted, thrusting open doors, searching for her family. "Where are you? Answer me!" she screamed.

Bernadette ran through the house, searching for her family. There was no sign of them anywhere.

Bernadette was terrified.

"It's a lie!"

Choking through her tears and screams, she looked everywhere with a feverish intensity.

"WHERE ARE YOU!"

Bernadette cried until she was too exhausted to go any further. Collapsing in a corner, she put her hands over her face and huddled, wary, and dazed for hours.

It was nearing midnight when she lifted her head and snapped open her eyes. After standing, she glanced down at the body. Her clothes spattered in blood. Bernadette began to adjust her skirt neatly and pat her hair back into place. Bernadette walked toward the kitchen.

Now midnight, Bernadette was frustrated at herself serving dinner so late, but it was finally on the table. A charred, blackened roast sat near the head of the table.

The bloodied carving knife lay neatly beside a pitcher of iced tea. The mangled body of Dr. Walsh sat wedged tightly against the table beside her. Her glassy frozen eyes stared upward; her head hung awkwardly over one shoulder. Blood oozed through the cloth table napkin neatly tucked in place at Dr. Walsh's neckline. Bernadette spoke in a quiet, low-pitched whisper.

"I'm so glad we had our little talk, doctor. I am delighted you were able to stay and join us for dinner. Children, tell Dr. Walsh how happy you are to have her join us."

Bernadette rested her elbows on the table. Her eyes took on a strange, sullen appearance. A twisted grin distorted her face, and her voice became childlike, sweet, almost infantile.

"It's very nice to have you here, Dr. Walsh," Bernadette mimics Chelsea's voice. Her tone changes into the pitch of a small boy. "It sure is!"

"As you can see, everything is perfect now. I won't be visiting you in the future, and you see, there is no need for you to worry. Isn't that right, darling?"

Bernadette turned from the disheveled, bloody body of Dr. Walsh. She blew a kiss across the table toward the empty seat. Her expression crazed, her grin even more distorted. There was a thick throaty tone to her voice now, a deep unnatural sound as though it had dredged up from hell.

"That's right, Dr. Walsh. My wife has great confidence in you, but as you can see, everything is perfect!"

12

THE LAST BUBBLE

The bus stopped at the corner of 42nd Street and Lancaster Avenue at 8:45 a.m. Just like it had the day before and the day before that. A daily routine for Charlie Lewis, leaving him ten minutes to walk the two blocks up 42nd Street to Bradford's Collection Agency. Enough time to get to work and clock in before 9:00 a.m. Charlie had worked for Mr. Bradford for the past nine years, and Bradford did not like tardiness.

Charlie could only remember one time when he was late. When the bus driver, Willie O'Connor, who had driven that route for more than fifteen years, died at the wheel. Heart attack.

Poor old Willie thought Charlie.

Charlie had a lot of respect for Willie, who was solely dedicated to his work. Willie reminded Charlie of himself.

The new bus driver was a long-haired hippie, who was very unfriendly, except when it came to girls. Always flirting and not paying enough attention to the road. He had a couple of near misses over the past years. Charlie didn't like him much.

The door of the bus slammed open. Charlie stepped into a crowd of waiting riders, anxious to beat the others to any seats. As Charlie stepped down onto the sidewalk, his right foot landed on a gob of chewing gum.

Charlie became livid as he scuffed the sole of his foot against the ground while he walked along 42nd Street. Charlie hated bubble gum. He hated any kind of gum.

Charlie was a quiet, soft-spoken short man, five feet, three inches standing. When he was young, the kids would always tease him. Charlie was the only one who couldn't blow chewing gum bubbles in his class, and his classmates used every opportunity to make his life miserable. They would put gum in his chair and then laugh at the gum stuck to his derriere for the rest of the day. Bubble gum always reminded him of those unhappy childhood days. He recalled the time they stuffed wads of chewing gum into his backpack and sealed his favorite book shut by inserting chewed gum throughout the pages.

Once, during a sleepover, someone put bubble gum in his hair while he slept. The next day, his mom had to shave him bald. Charlie walked around humiliated for three months until his hair grew back.

When Charlie reached the Bradford Building entrance, he thought he'd scraped most of the gum from his shoe. As he walked the two flights of stairs to his work area, he could still feel his sole sticking slightly to the surface.

"Good morning, Mr. Lewis. Mr. Bradford would like to see you in his office," said Jenny, one of the newer secretaries. Her voice was shrill and high pitched. Charlie rarely responded to her in hopes that she would not say anything else.

As Jenny handed Charlie his mail, he noticed a thick wad of chewed bubble gum stuck to the rim of her coffee cup. He cringed as he headed towards Mr. Bradford's office.

"Come in, Charlie," Bradford bellowed. He was a big, burly fellow in his early sixties. A cunning businessman, Bradford had turned a small car repo business into a multi-million-dollar venture. He enjoyed sapping the life out of simple people; those living day to day on shoestring budgets, unable to pay their bills or meet their mortgages. He had expanded his business over the past few years to foreclosing homes, land, businesses, and hope.

Bradford leaned forward and cleared his throat. His eyes were more deliberate now. "I'll get to the point quickly, Charlie. I've noticed a remarkable increase in your volume of accounts receivables over the past year." He mopped his brow and cleared his throat once again. Bradford spoke loudly.

"Good work, my man! Good work! The Bradford Collection Agency could use more men like you."

"Thank you, sir," said Charlie. Bradford smiled broadly. Reaching into his top desk drawer, he pulled out a pack of chewing gum.

"Care for a stick, Charlie?" he said insistently, thrusting his colossal arm forward.

Charlie winced as he shook his head, "No, thank you, sir."

By the end of the day, Charlie had finalized the paperwork on three separate residential home foreclosures and had entered default filings on two small business loans. It had been a good day for Charlie. Mr. Bradford would be proud.

"Goodnight, Mr. Lewis," said Jenny, her voice chirping.

Charlie didn't even look back. He could hear Jenny popping the bubble gum as he walked out the door. Her mouth gaped wide open with each chew. The thought of it as the same piece of gum he noticed on the rim of her coffee cup earlier that morning made him sick to his stomach.

The bus ride home was uncomfortable. Charlie closed his eyes for a moment. As the bus neared its next stop, he opened his eyes and glanced to his right. A small boy leaned over the back of the seat opposite him; his eyes fixed on Charlie. He had a wad of bubble gum stretched between his two hands. The boy beamed as though he awaited applause after performing a successful magic trick. Charlie noticed how dirty the little boy's hands were as he rolled the gum up and popped it back into his mouth.

Charlie wanted to puke. He rolled his eyes and quickly turned his head to survey the passing crowd along the sidewalk. Looking up, he caught the sight of an old abandoned billboard; you could barely make out the word 'Double.' The rest of the billboard was faded and tattered, but there was an image of a package of chewing gum and the faint word 'Pleasure.'

"Ugh," he scowled to himself.

Charlie was glad when the bus finally arrived at his stop. The traffic had been bumper-to-bumper, and the ride home was long and exhausting.

As Charlie departed the bus, he glanced back at the little boy. Now hanging in a long thin line from the child's mouth, the gum spun in full circles. Charlie felt faint.

It was a three-block walk to Charlie's house. As he neared his home, he noticed a woman kneeling beside a small child just ahead of him.

"Open your mouth," he could hear her say. "Open your mouth. Let me see. Did you swallow your gum? I told you not to swallow your gum."

The child stood innocently unresponsive. Charlie could see the woman's face.

"See," she said. "This is how you do it." She reminded Charlie of a cow chewing cud. Her exaggerated motions ended with her saying in a garbled tone, "Then... you spit it out... like this!" A big lump of gum landed beside Charlie's foot.

"Oops!" she said as Charlie clumsily jerked his foot sideways to avoid stepping on it.

"Sorry," she mumbled, embarrassed.

Charlie sneered as he passed. He resented all the children in the neighborhood. Always running up and down the street, screaming and shouting. Doing all the things children always do, like playing.

Charlie hated all the noise they made. He didn't like bubble gum, and he didn't like children, either.

He passed Mr. and Mrs. Emerson's house. The couple had been together for over thirty years; the home was their wedding gift to themselves. The house stood empty now, forced to move last week. Charlie was credited with the foreclosure procedures on that one, too.

Three houses away, his small two-bedroom home stood atop a high ceiling storage basement. It took twenty steps to reach the front porch. His was the only house in the neighborhood with that many stairs. The kids loved jumping off his front steps, which infuriated Charlie.

There they were again. "Get out of my yard!" he said as he approached his lawn. "You brats, go play somewhere else!"

"Get a life, fart face!" shouted one of the boys.

"Yeah!" said another, while the other children giggled as they all scrambled away.

Charlie grumbled as he climbed the stairs. Inside, he nestled into the couch to relax in front of the television. The room appeared dark and dismal. The dingy walls, worn navy furnishings, and gray shag carpeting covering the entire floor added to its shabby appearance. Accessories were absent, except for a few old pillows at the end of the couch. He yawned and clicked the remote control to a movie that featured a handsome young couple.

Charlie took off his shoes and peeled off his socks. The odor from his aching feet caused him to be taken aback for a moment. Charlie thought how pretty the young woman on the television was. The couple was scantily clad, and Charlie became aroused as he watched the man run his fingers across the woman's firm body. The man placed his hand to the woman's lips. Charlie could not quite hear what they were saying. The children's laughter was loud in the background.

"Brats!" Charlie said.

Charlie continued to stare into the TV set, flinching as he watched the young man take a piece of gum from the woman's mouth and place it in his. They kissed.

Charlie was utterly distraught by their actions, leaning forward to stop the rush of blood flowing to his head. Within moments, the sound of the living room picture window shattering caused his head to snap up so quickly that he was slightly off-balance when he stood up from the couch. Charlie promptly picked up the baseball as he fumbled to jerk open the front door. Charlie ran out onto the porch.

"Stay right there, you brats!" He screamed at the children as they laughed and ran in all directions. "Your parents are going to pay for that window!"

"Drop dead, you dumb shit!" A voice yelled from a distance. It was the same annoying voice from earlier, the same annoying child on his porch when he arrived home. From the corner of his eye, Charlie saw the boy dart from behind a parked car.

As Charlie turned toward the boy's direction, he could see the kid reach into his mouth and pull out a big wad of gum. Grasping it and aiming as though he was readying a weapon.

Charlie began to lunge across the porch. He was determined to catch the culprit and not let him escape. As his foot hit the top step, the boy slung the wad of gum forcefully in Charlie's direction.

Charlie's eyes focused on the wet blob plummeting toward him. It seemed to glide in slow motion as it neared. All Charlie could do was stare at the wad coming his way. As he did so, his mind quickly flashed to his childhood days.

Charlie's classmates were laughing and teasing him. He could see himself crying as he tried to pull the gum off the bottom of his pants. His head jerked about as his mother cut chewing gum out of his hair. He trembled as he recalled the sound of laughter rising loudly around him.

Charlie's fingers tightened around the baseball. As he raised his arm to throw it, the gum landed on the step, just under his barefoot, lodging between his big toe and second toe. Spastically, his toes wrapped around the wet mass of gum.

When Charlie felt the moist, sticky lump, he thrust his foot upward uncontrollably, causing him to lose his balance and tumble headfirst down the flight of stairs. The hard, dull, thumping sound of his body falling down the stairs frightened the boy. He turned and ran so fast that he was halfway down the street by the time Charlie's body hit the base of the stairs. Charlie lay still, inanimate, with a fractured skull and broken neck.

His death was instant.

It was a beautiful Saturday afternoon, less than one year after Charlie's untimely death. The neighboring lawns cluttered with giggling children at play. Charlie's home wore a completely new exterior. The grass was green and vibrant, with newly planted and brightly covered flowering blooms lining the walkway to the front steps.

Inside the freshly painted Lewis home, a young couple trotted behind real estate agent Ester Parsons.

"This is a charming neighborhood. Perfect for families," Ester Parsons continued. "There are lots of playmates for children, as you can see, and there's a school just around the corner. I might add it is a highly rated school as well. Are you planning to have children anytime soon?"

The young couple glanced at one another with coy grins spread across their faces. "I'm pregnant now," blushed the young woman.

"Well... That is wonderful. Congratulations!" said Ester Parsons.

"Wow... this house just seems too good to be true, and the price is perfect," the man said, his tone a bit curious.

"It is a lovely little house for the price. You won't find anything else like it within miles," responded Ester Parsons.

Turning towards Ester Parsons, he asked, "Why did the owner decide to sell?"

"Well... unfortunately, he had a little accident. He died suddenly, but nothing to concern yourself with," replied Ms. Parsons.

"Oh, it's just perfect for us," squealed the young woman as she embraced her husband's arm with hers. "Don't you think so, honey?" Taking a deep breath, she continued, "And, my gosh... it smells so good. Umm, do you smell that honey?"

"Yeah... it does smell good. Fresh paint?" the young man asked Ester Parsons.

"It sure is! I think it's called Bubblegum Pink."

13

BLOODY MARY

Bloody Mary is her name. Bloody Mary is the game.
Martin Boylan was not only the class clown, but he was the
class bully, too. A teacher's worse nightmare was how Mr.
Wesley, one of his 7th-grade teachers, described him, and
Martin was the first to admit he could create a few problems.
When asked why he was always causing trouble, Martin
simply smiled sarcastically and replied, "Hell if I know!"

Tyrone's mother was the only person he seemed to show
any respect for. Maybe it was because he somehow knew
she wouldn't take any stuff. Tyrone was Martin's best friend
when they weren't fighting.

Martin was thirteen years old. He recently returned to
school after a five-day suspension for stabbing his classmate,

Josie, with a pencil. Martin swore it was an accident. He claimed they were playing 'five finger fillet and that Josie was all in on the fun. Martin said the game required Josie to place her hand on the table palm down with her fingers spread apart and that he jabbed his pencil between her fingers. Martin claimed Josie had played the game many times before, but this time she moved her fingers.

"If I had tried to do it, it woulda been a lot worse! You woulda been taking her to the hospital!"

Except Josie swore, Martin had forcefully pressed her hand against the table.

"He jabbed a sharpened pencil between my fingers," she explained to the principal.

Josie said she screamed as the pencil pierced through her middle finger. There was blood everywhere. Josie did not get suspended.

Martin thought Josie was funny-looking. She had silver braces on both her upper and lower teeth and freckles all over her face and neck. Martin didn't learn anything from the past when kids teased him for his braces when he was nine years old. Instead, he turned his anger at Josie.

Martin had already called Mr. Wesley every name in the book, but Wesley felt there was no need to send Martin back to the principal's office. He knew he would just cut school on his way to the office like he had done so many times before. Besides, Mr. Wesley felt there was a kind spot somewhere in Martin and wanted to help bring it out. He knew Martin wanted to be in class. He was a smart kid who, over the past year, started falling behind. No one knew why.

Plus, Martin loved to generate giggles from his peers from the back of the room.

Martin would purposely stand in the rear of the room, placing himself in the corner when Mr. Wesley would attempt to rebuke his actions. He would stand there comically, miming like a clown jester for even more laughs. His clowning did not stop; it continued whether he was standing or sitting. The only thing missing was the costume. Martin was in the back of the room when Mr. Wesley spoke.

"Take your seat, Martin, and don't let me hear another word from you." Mr. Wesley spoke sternly above the background chuckles.

Martin coolly strolled back to his seat, mumbling under his breath." Yessa massa." The class roared.

Martin was wearing a white tee-shirt about three sizes too large with torn and very faded blue jeans. His family didn't have a lot of money, which had a lot to do with his attitude. He didn't want anyone to know that he was embarrassed by the way he dressed.

"Did you say something, Martin?" asked Mr. Wesley.

"Nope!" said Martin as he thumped down into his seat. Uncontrollable laughter filled the room.

"Quiet down! Clear off your desk and get ready for lunch. Everyone! Now! Be prepared to take this week's history exam when I see you in class tomorrow. Those of you, and you know who you are, might be smart to use your time wisely to study."

Martin was the first one seated at their regular lunch bench.

He had cut the lunch line and was nearly finished with his lunch when his classmates joined him.

"Man, how come you didn't save me a place in line?" said Tyrone annoyingly.

"Every man to himself," said Martin, "You got to do your own cutting."

Donald, Linda, Alex, and Sharon soon joined the table. Sharon and Linda were the two most popular girls in the seventh grade, and the cutest too. At least that's what Martin thought. He admired Sharon, but he just didn't know how to act when you liked a girl as cute as Sharon. Martin imagined trying some of the sexy things on the internet with her but decided not to. At least not yet, he thought to himself, giggling with a kind of half-smile as Sharon settled into the bench beside him. Besides, Martin didn't know for sure how Sharon felt about him. She never gave him any signals that might let him know whether she felt the same way. She didn't look at him in the same way as a few of the uglier girls looked at him, like Josie.

"Yuk," he whispered at the thought of kissing Josie.

Plus, Sharon sure was pretty. *She was beautiful.* He found himself almost thinking aloud.

"Martin... Martin," Sharon repeated, nudging Martin out of his daydreaming. "Why'd you stick Josie with that pencil? That was wrong," she said, scolding gently.

"How many times I got to say it was an accident," snapped Martin.

"Didn't your momma teach you that you're not supposed to hit girls... that includes stabbing them with your pencil,"

Linda said snidely.

"Who said?" asked Donald, "I'd hit your mamma if she hit me first."

"You wouldn't hit Tyrone's momma," giggled Linda. "Remember that time she chased you up the street when you badmouthed her? I just knew you were gonna die that day."

"Yeah, Tyrone, that was hella funny; yo mamma was all up in Donald's face. Yo mamma be tripping," said Martin. "Don't talk about my mama, man," snapped Tyrone.

"Damn, what's up with you, fool? Can't you take a joke?" replied Martin.

Tyrone's cell phone rang. He reached into his pocket and pulled it out. "Hello. Yeah, momma, I will. I'll be home on time, momma," he whispered, quickly dismissing the call.

Martin let out a loud laugh, "Damn, man!"

"You know Josie likes you. Everybody knows it. That's why she keeps messing with you," said Sharon.

"Yeah, man, maybe you can get you a matching pair of braces," laughed Tyrone. Everybody at the table began to laugh, and Martin tried to hide his embarrassment. As the group continued to laugh, Martin picked up a baby carrot off Sharon's food tray and threw it at the next table. The carrot hit Josie on the right side of her head. Everyone at both tables burst out in loud laughter. Of course, Josie didn't think it was funny. The truth is that Josie had lied. She wanted to play 'five finger fillet' with Martin.

They all finished eating their lunch except for Alex. Alex always ate slow and was regularly the last to finish his meal.

"What do you want to do now?" asked Donald.

"We could study for our history exam," said Alex.

Everyone turned to look at Alex. "What's up with you, man?" asked Martin, "You stupid or something?"

Alex slumped down in his seat. He was a long way from stupid. He was one of the smartest kids in the school, and everyone knew it. So bright that he was nicknamed Worm, short for bookworm because of his thick bifocals and his intellectual manner. Alex was frail and a lot smaller than the rest of his classmates, which probably had a lot to do with the nickname. Alex genuinely wanted to fit in and be accepted by the group. He was grateful to hang out with what he considered the most popular kids in his grade, even though he knew they were using him. His homework was copied regularly by everyone at the table, except for Sharon. But Alex did not care about being taken advantage of. He wanted to belong at whatever the cost and would do anything to be considered a part of the group.

Linda pulled a compact from her purse and started touching up her lips with a shiny red gloss.

"Check this out," said Martin, looking directly at Linda.

"Did you know that the devil's wife is in the mirror?"

"Man, you the one that's crazy... not Alex!" declared Donald loudly.

"Do I look crazy, fool?" Martin shouted.

Having a delayed reaction to Martin's comment, Linda dropped her compact and shrieked, "In what mirror?"

"In any mirror, including yours," replied Martin. "Her name's Bloody Mary."

"Man, you full of it!" Donald sneered.

"No!" blurted Tyrone. "I heard about Bloody Mary a long time ago. It's a game. My cousin told me about it."

"It ain't no game, fool!" shouted Martin. "Why don't you just shut up! Every time I say something, you always come up talking about you done heard it, you done seen it, or you done did it! ... Anyway, do you guys want to hear this or not?"

"Yeah," Tyrone said, quietly defeated. The others nodded in unison.

Martin began to speak in a deep, hushed whisper. "So, listen... If you walk up to a mirror in a dark room, splash some water on the mirror, and then say B-l-o-o-d-y M-a-r-y four times, she'll come out!"

"Come out and do what?" asked Linda as she carefully recovered her compact from the ground.

"Get you, I guess!" Martin added with a shrug.

"How do you know?" Donald asked sarcastically.

"I just know!"

"Yeah, right!" said Donald.

"Listen, everybody," insisted Tyrone once again. "My cousin really did tell me about this game last year. It happened to a friend of his, Marisa. She kept talking about playing the game. One day she came up missing, and when they found her, her brain was gone. Her head was flat as a doormat."

Sharon winced at the thought, "That's awful!"

"That's bullshit!" said Donald.

"Well, I don't believe it," Linda said flatly, continuing to put the finishing touches on her lips as she resumed staring into her compact. "I don't believe any of it!"

"I bet you'd believe that bible upside yo' head if yo' mamma caught you with all that shit on your lips and that short skirt showing all yo' ass! Everybody knows you change your clothes before and after school," Martin said snidely.

Linda was visibly angry at Martin's comment but more embarrassed that everyone knew she was sneaking and changing her clothes before and after school.

Alex pushed his food aside and asked, "But... what if... what if she does come out... then what?"

Martin quickly responded, "Then you're just dead! 'Cept, if you turn the lights back on really quick before she comes all the way out of the mirror, she'll go away."

"Stop lying, man. I knew you were crazy," mocked Donald as he maliciously discounted Martin's comments by waving his hands through the air.

"I ain't lying, and I'll prove it," said Martin growing increasingly angrier.

"Why would anybody want to see the devil's wife, anyway?" Sharon asked. "I wouldn't."

"Just something to do, I guess," said Martin.

"How do you know the devil even has a wife?" asked Alex.

"How do you know he doesn't?" responded Martin.

"Well, I don't want anything to do with it," said Sharon.

"Me either," said Alex, sinking still lower into his seat.

"What's the matter? Chickens? You both got yellow streaks running down your backs!" Donald smirked.

"I'm not chicken," Alex quickly chimed in, straightening up in his seat.

"Well... I'm not interested," said Sharon.

"Ah, come on, Sharon, I wanna see. Anyway, it is only a game," said Linda, still embarrassed but wanting to make sure the attention was no longer on her. She snapped her compact shut and licked her lips seductively.

"You been watching too much TV, bro!" said Donald.

Martin ignored Donald. "Yeah, Sharon, nothings gonna happen. Even the Worm wants to see," said Martin as the others chimed in unison, "Yeah, come on, Sharon!"

As Martin rose from the bench, the others simultaneously followed. Sharon was the last one seated but apprehensively rose and followed the others.

The bell seemed to ring forever, announcing the end of the lunch hour, as Martin and the others hid behind closed doors in the girl's bathroom on the third floor of the primary school building. The level was off-limits and heavily roped off. A fire had destroyed several of the classrooms resulting in significant smoke and water damage across the entire floor's interior, with renovation scheduled to begin during summer break. However, the area was an apparent hazard, and the students knew they were not supposed to be there.

The girl's bathroom had the least amount of damage, with only minor ash and charring. Martin peered out into the empty school hallway.

"So, this is what the girl's bathroom looks like," remarked Alex. Everyone broke out in laughter.

"Worm, you a real sissy," mocked Donald.

"Shut up," scolded Martin. "Somebody might hear. Be quiet. I want to make sure the hallway is clear." Martin peered through the small opening from behind the nearly closed door.

"Man, it's clear, ain't nobody supposed to be up here," Donald responded snidely.

"I can't get caught. My mom will kill me," said Sharon.

"Shhh..." said Martin.

Martin glanced up and down the corridor of the hallway before closing and latching the door. He pushed open the stall doors in the restroom to make sure nobody else was still inside.

Donald shook his head in disbelief. "Man, you stupid. You must think you're in a movie. Ain't nobody in those stalls."

Martin ignored Donald's comment stopping in front of the hand bowl farthest from the door. A large mirror stretched across the wall over six hand bowls. He waited for a moment longer and finally said, "Okay, everybody, the coast is clear. Come over here."

They all gathered around the sink basin except for Worm. Martin instructed Worm to stand by the light switch and turn it off and then on when told to do so. Alex eagerly agreed. He was thrilled to be given something to do. He liked the feeling of being included.

Martin took a step closer to the mirror.

"Listen up," he said with authority. "First, we have to fill the sink with water. Then," he added, "when I give the signal, everybody needs to grab up as much water as you can and splash it on the mirror. Then close your eyes, and when I count to three, we all have to say Bloody Mary together four times. Everybody has to say it, or it won't work, and you have to keep your eyes closed. Okay?"

Everyone nodded. Sharon less enthusiastically than the others. Martin told Linda to stuff paper toweling in the drain opening and fill the sink up with water.

As the water neared the top of the sink, Sharon said grimly, "I don't like this."

"It'll be all right," replied Martin, "Come stand by me. Okay, Worm, turn off the lights NOW!" Alex beamed as he diligently completed his first task.

"Oooh!" said Linda.

The restroom was windowless. The room was pitch-black and silent, except for the faint sound of the rusted ventilation fan overhead and Linda's occasional giggle.

"All right, everybody, start splashing the water onto the mirror."

Sharon reluctantly followed the others as the water slushed and splashed onto the mirror. Martin tilted his head back, directing his eyes upward. He wanted to be dramatic, even though no one could see what he was doing.

"Okay, everybody, close your eyes, and on the count of three, everybody has to say, 'Bloody Mary' four times. One Two Three!" As Martin began, the others chimed in rhythmic unison. "Bloody Mary! Bloody Mary! Bloody Mary!"

"Stop, Martin!" squealed Sharon, interrupting.

"Let's not stop now," Donald called out snidely. "I want

to see what this fool is gonna do next!"

"Come on, Sharon, it's just a game," said a giggling Linda.

"Okay, on three. One, Two, Three! Bloody Mary!"

"Now open your eyes," said Martin.

They all waited in silence for a few moments in the darkness, staring at the mirror. Nothing happened.

"I told you guys that Martin was full of it. Man, you have gone stupid on us," taunted Donald.

"We broke the chant. We might need to do it again without stopping," said Martin.

"I'm not doing this again," said Sharon, "Alex, turn on the lights."

"Not yet, Alex, don't turn them on yet!" Martin shouted at Alex.

"What's that smell?" asked Linda.

"This is a bathroom... you know... toilets," mocked Donald, holding his nose. A strong, foul odor began to seep up from one of the stalls.

"What's that?" Sharon asked abruptly in a whispery, hushed tone. "Did you hear that?"

A quiet clanking sound also seemed to be coming from the area of the stalls.

"It's just the fan," said Tyrone.

Linda glanced toward the mirror. There was a little glare, barely noticeable near the center, two pin-sized spots of light. Her mouth flew open. "Look! Look at the mirror," Linda said excitedly.

Everyone stared at the mirror.

At that moment, the pin-sized lights in the mirror began to grow slowly, transforming into what appeared to be two illuminating eyes, manifesting like magic right before them. Even Donald gasped quietly under his breath; he too became frightened and could not move. None of them could. The clanking in the background began to grow louder while faint sobbing echoes began to fill the room. The eyes seem to peer out from the mirror as they continued to grow larger and larger, feeding off the energy drawn from their frightened eyes. Suddenly droplets of blood began to flow from the eyes in the mirror.

"Oh, shit!" said Donald.

"Stop it, Martin!" screamed Sharon, "Alex, turn on the lights!"

The mirror began to crack as the faint image of a woman's head started to form around the eyes. Linda screamed, dropping her purse to the floor. Her compact shattered as it rolled from the bag and under the sink.

The cracks began to cover the mirror more quickly—the room filled with the putrid smell of foul urine. The eyes stared menacingly upon the group of young people. The face of a woman was now fully visible. It was a face filled with pure evil. The glow from her eyes began to form flames which shot like fireballs from the mirror, filling the room with enormous heat and painfully blinding light. Blood gushed from the mirror. Sharon could barely call out to Alex; she was overwhelmed by fear. Everything happened so suddenly; they were all stricken with angst and terror.

The image of the woman was now complete. Her entire body was frighteningly evil. She was nude and drenched in blood. The devil's wife emerged from beyond the dimensions of hell. Her movement was quick and jerky. You could hear long, low moans coming from her. Everyone started to scream.

"Worm!" Martin yelled, stuttering as he tried to get the words out, "Turn on the light! Worm, turn on the light now! Worm! Worm! Worm!" The sounds of multiple screams filled the entire bathroom.

That evening, the parents reached out to the local police department to report that their children did not come home. Officers visited the homes and took reports. After realizing that the teens were missing together, the consensus was that they were likely out together and would make their way back home later that night. Except they did not.

The following morning the families gathered at the police station. Tyrone's mother was loud in her anger and insisted that someone do something to immediately locate their children. A county-wide search quickly launched.

When Tyrone's mother mentioned that she had spoken to him by phone the previous afternoon, the detective assigned to the case ordered the tracking of the phone's last location. The last time-stamped cell sight ping locale was the afternoon of the previous day on the school campus.

A swarm of officers deployed to search the school. The police searched the entire campus before discovering the shocking scene on the third level in the girl's bathroom. The floor appeared seeped in colored water as though a fire had been doused in a dense red wine. Thick sticky blood was everywhere. A purse and mirror compact laid open beneath the sink basin furthest from the door. The large glass mirror above the line of sink basins billowed with spider cracks.

An officer opened a toilet stall door and stumbled backward, nearly falling into the reddened water.

"Oh my God," he cried out as a second officer rushed over and peered into the stall.

"Secure the scene now!" The second officer screamed into his hand radio. "Code 55-A! Code 55-A! We need the forensic team out here now. Notify the chief immediately!"

Martin's head was floating in the urine and stool stained toilet bowl like a bled-out bobblehead. Drizzled blood spats covered his tormented face. The second officer immediately began to kick open each of the stalls. As he gasped loudly in horror.

Behind each door was the head of each student, bobbing in claret red blood-stained toilet bowls.

"Where are the bodies?" The first officer wailed loudly, coughing through tears. "Where are the bodies?" He cried.

It was a week before school reopened. The tardy bell rang as loud as usual. Mr. Wesley completed roll call and instructed the class to pull out their history books.

"Turn to chapter thirty-two for a final review. The quiz on this chapter will begin in thirty-minutes," said Mr.

Wesley, staring out unemotionally at the group of groaning students.

"And," he continued, "I hope most of you do a lot better than you did on the last test," he said, continuing. "Before we get started, let us have a moment of silence. It was a tragedy that befell some of our students and our school. I know a few of you were close friends with them. What happened is scary and stressful, so I also want to remind you that counselors are on hand if you need to talk to someone. In the meantime, let's keep them in our prayers. Please close your eyes for a moment."

A tear slowly rolled down Josie's face as she glanced at Martin's empty seat. The students sat silent for a few moments.

"Okay, get those books out. You only have a short while before the exam," remarked Mr. Wesley.

Thirty minutes later.

"Alex!" called Mr. Wesley. "Come, pass out the exams."

Alex's expression appeared haunted, unfocused. He sat hunched down in his chair like a tiny baby waiting to be coddled. Riddled with guilt, *They were right, they were all right*, he thought to himself. *I am a coward, a worm.*

Alex was always scared. He always had been and always would be. Growing up, Alex was afraid of everything. Nightmares, shadows, the boogeyman, and especially the dark. It was the darkness that had always frightened Alex the most.

He felt the warmth of the rush of blood traveling to his head, becoming faint as he recalled the abject fear that had overwhelmed him the day they ventured into the third-floor bathroom. He thought he had outgrown his fearfulness. When Alex turned out the lights, he panicked. He was so frightened that while everyone closed their eyes and chanted "Bloody Mary," he snuck out the darkened room.

Alex didn't think it was real. He simply thought everyone would laugh about it. They would just call him 'Worm' like they always did. But, when the room went dark, his anxiety and fears immediately returned, and his act of desertion now seized and repulsed him with despairing shame. It was as though he was still crouched powerless in the corner at the end of the corridor, immobilized by the frightening, faint cries of his classmates coming from behind the closed restroom doors. Screams so horrifying that he could still feel the shivering vibrations in the core of his soul.

No one would believe me, even if I were to tell. Plus, what would everyone think of me? I couldn't live with myself if they knew how I snuck out of the bathroom. No one would understand how I was too scared to move or call for help.

"Alex! Alex!" Mr. Wesley called out, "What's wrong with you? Are you ill?" Alex, still benumbed, could not murmur a whisper.

"Here," Mr. Wesley said, holding the exam paperwork in his hand and extending his arm impatiently in Alex's direction. "Pass these test papers out quickly. I need to make sure you all have enough time to complete your exam. Once you finish the test, I'll write you up a hall pass if you think you need to see the school counselor."

14

SANDCASTLE

A deep moat surrounded the castle. It was a magnificent and massive fortress with thick walls and huge pillars. The only entry to the castle was across the drawbridge, which was, for the moment, drawn to keep intruders out. There was an array of buildings behind the towering walls of the castle. The Great Hall, where all would gather to laugh, sing, and dance, and the Ladies Chamber, a private, luxurious space for pampering and sleeping, were Johanna's favorite rooms.

The damp sand was soothing against Johanna's fingers as she gently pressed the moistened stone-like moldings, carefully tending the finishing touches on the castle sculpted of sand.

Johanna spent the past few weeks building the sandcastle on the isolated beach just footsteps from the home she shared with her husband of five years. The likeness to an authentic medieval castle was uncanny. Sculpting and watching over her castle had become a daily escape for Johanna.

Her husband, Phillip, an investment banker, was born into wealth. An only child, he savored the attention reaped upon him by parents, who gave him nearly everything he wanted as a trade-off for quiet, undisturbed behavior. As Phillip grew to manhood, he also grew to expect the same from life. He settled only for the best, the most expensive, the most beautiful. Johanna was beautiful.

To Johanna, Phillip was the prince charming she had always dreamt of and desired. He was educated, handsome, he was wealthy. Everything about him was immaculate, from the clothes he wore, how he maintained his body, to the six-bedroom home they shared on the beachfront. When Phillip asked her to marry him, it was her fairy tale come true.

We were meant to be together, so Johanna thought, until that day, the first time he hit her. That was three years ago, and nothing was ever the same after that day. After that moment, Johanna lived her days on the edge of fear, never knowing what to expect or when to expect it.

She had become accustomed to hiding her emotions, masking her fear behind forced, insincere smiles. She was even more adept at her pretense of sensations of love with a partner who no longer made her feel safe and protected.

Johanna clutched tightly to her emotions, carefully minding her responses, managing her words, never talking back.

She made every effort to avoid the unwarranted wrath that revealed itself with his anger.

Born a twin to her sister Julia, Johanna's parents and her sister died in a tragic car accident when she was a small child. From that day on, she was passed from foster family to foster family until age seventeen when she became emancipated.

Once on her own, she worked long hours to put herself through college, leaving no time for friends. While her parent's memory faded over time, she longed for Julia. The loss of her twin sister imposed a sense of grief that was always with her.

Feeling lonely was not new to Johanna. Since her family's death, there had never really been anyone to share her joy or pain.

Johanna's toes sank into the sand as she sat comforted by the gentle ocean breezes floating across the purple bruises on her face. The sandcastle was a peaceful retreat during the hours that Phillip was away at work. The time spent on the secluded beach was liberating freedom, even if only for a little while. These were moments when Johanna could fantasize about existence so different than the reality of the life she was now living. The world within the walls of her sandcastle was a beautiful illusion, far removed from the certainty of the nightmare that awaited her daily.

The Great Hall radiated with laughter, alive with music and dancing. Jesters, jugglers, and acrobats leaped about entertaining the boisterous onlookers as food passed around the room.

Johanna sat near the end of a long table filled with aunts, uncles, cousins, and twin sister Julia. Her mother, Lady Margaret, sat beside her, radiant and full of chatter.

"Johanna darling, is it true that Mary Grace is barren?"

"I have not heard, mother, but be it a blessing rather than a curse. Her husband, Lord Bryon, is dreadfully ugly," replied Johanna snidely.

"Ugly," shouted her sister Julia, "Their babies would easily be mistaken for wild boars." Loud laughter filled the room.

"Barren is certainly a curse that I would not wish on my worst enemy," remarked Lady Margaret. "A woman is not a woman if she cannot bear a child. But I must admit they both are quite ugly, indeed."

Johanna's head flopped back as she roared with laughter with the others, her golden hair loosely brushing beneath her shoulders. Johanna was relaxed and happy within her castle walls.

"My lady," a voice whispered, going unheard over the laughter and lively prattle.

Inside her castle, life was glorious. Johanna languished in wealth and pampering, surrounded by her family. Johanna smiled as she watched the others overflowing with laughter. Here, life was beautiful.

"My lady," the servant repeated as he leaned near to Johanna's ear. "Lord Commodus awaits your company in the bower. Shall you join him?" He quietly spoke as he filled her goblet with aged wine.

Johanna reached for the drinking vessel to hide the devilish grin fixed across her lips. As she sipped, she envisioned Lord Commodus quietly slipping into the bower unnoticed, her private room, intended for the use of her ladyship only.

She turned back to the servant beside her.

"Tell Lord Commodus that there will be no rest for him tonight," she whispered, unabashed.

Replying with a quick nod of his head, he promptly moved to fill Lady Margaret's goblet before preparing to depart from the hall.

"Good lad," remarked Lady Margaret to the servant as she lifted her flowing goblet into the air. Her lighthearted words continued as he disappeared from the great hall.

"Wine soothes the soul, muddles the brain, and makes ugly things look beautiful. A toast to Mary Grace and Lord Byron. May their thirst for wine be eternal so that they never know how ugly they both truly are!"

The great hall roared with the sound of laughter.

The night was still. Johanna is comforted in the arms of Lord Commodus as he lay sleeping beside her. She wished the night would never end. As she snuggled in closer to his warm body, the sound of waves grew louder and louder in the background.

Johanna awoke from her fleeting thoughts. The sand was cold against her body and had dampened her clothing. It was nearing dusk, and the rush of the tide brought her back to her reality. Realizing the lateness, Johanna began to panic; dinner had to be on the table before Phillip arrived home.

Phillip was Johanna's first love. She was in her final year of college when they met six years ago. Yet, it felt more like a lifetime had passed since those days. *How things had changed,* she thought to herself as she raced back to the house. Johanna knew Phillip had been with other women, and no matter what she did, she could no longer satisfy him. Everything she did was wrong.

While putting the finishing touches on dinner, Johanna wondered if Phillip still loved her, equally questioning her feelings.

How do you love someone you are now afraid of loving? She thought to herself. It was even worse when Phillip drank. His anger was explosive, and she feared that if he drank too much or got too angry, he might kill her. He had become increasingly violent, and his abuse had grown increasingly worse.

If you look closely, you could see the weary tension buried beneath Johanna's eyes, but she was still alluring. Her beauty radiated past her bruised swollen eye and darkened blood-crusted lip.

The house sat five-hundred yards from the shoreline overlooking the ocean on an isolated stretch of beachfront. Most people would view it as a piece of heaven carved from the sky. It was magnificent in appearance, but for Johanna, it was misleading and likened to a castle dungeon, one incarcerating the solely innocent.

That evening, Phillip beat Johanna.

She mistakenly spilled a drop of red wine while refilling Phillip's glass. After the beating, Phillip made drunken love to her that same night.

The following morning, after Phillip left for work, Johanna heedfully completed her chores, eager to rush down to the sandcastle. The beachfront and her castle were the places she felt most content, escaping into a world void of hurt and pain for hours. Happily immersed in her imagination.

That night, she moved about on pins and needles, hoping to spare herself from Phillip's nightly beating once he arrived home. She lucked out. It was nearly 3:00 a.m. in the morning when Phillip came home with the aromatic sweetness of another woman oozing from his body. He was dazed and half-conscious in his drunken stupor. Johanna was surprised that he even made it home.

For a moment, Johanna envisioned his car missing the turn on the roadway and barreling into a tree. She quickly wrestled the thought from her head to remember a time when she genuinely loved Phillip. Even in her pain, she did not wish him dead; she only sought a safe escape.

The sound of joyous singing and laughter filled the room. Johanna sat in celebration, surrounded by her entire family. The young servant again leaned over and whispered in her ear.

"Lord Commodus awaits you, my Lady."

Beyond the whispers, the truth was that most knew of the amorous relationship between Johanna and Lord Commodus.

Moments later, Johanna was wrapped tightly in the warmth of his arms. As Johanna rested beside Lord Commodus, she was startled suddenly by the crashing sound of immense waves and wind. The sky began to darken out the moonlight, and the winds whip through the room, diminishing the candlelights which permeated the space. Johanna awakened Lord Commodus.

"What is it... what is happening? Are the gods angry at us?" she asked Commodus.

"No, my darling. The gods could never be angry at us. Come closer to me, close your eyes. I shall protect you. I shall love you. A joyous life awaits us, and we shall forever be together."

Suddenly a flood of ocean waves rushed through the castle. The surge was strong, powerful. Strangely, the furnishings remained in place against the massive rush of water. Johanna could hear laughter and singing in the background as the water filled the room, rising to the bed's level and continuing to engulf the couple.

"Lord Commodus," Johanna worriedly called his name.

"Shhh...Worry not, my darling, instead let us embrace. Hold on to me tightly, Johanna."

The water rose to the ceiling. Through the murky, watery darkness, Johanna and Lord Commodus held tightly to one another.

That evening, the shoreline was eerily calm. A massive wave had crested upon the shore. Remnants of the sandcastle remained, with walls tumbled and washed away as sand mixed with the cold seawater, spilling throughout the castle walls.

The following morning voices screamed out Johanna's name as the police and search party stretched along the beach. Phillip, accompanied by the police chief, walked past the remains of the toppled sandcastle.

"What is this? The chief asked.

"Nothing," responded Phillip, "Just Johanna's careless use of time. She was never one to manage her day consistently." Phillip sighed. "This is so unlike Johanna. God, please let her be all right."

As they continued along the shorefront, Phillip halted suddenly.

"What is it? Is something wrong?" asked the chief.

"I thought I heard something."

"Like what? I didn't hear anything."

"I don't know... I guess it was just the wind."

Phillip peered out across the shoreline. The water stretched as far as he could see. The ripples of tiny waves crawled close to his feet. The sulfur smell of the ocean was strong and lingering.

"Probably just the seagulls circling above," remarked the police chief.

"Yeah... probably," responded Phillip.

They continued down the shoreline.

As the months passed, you could often see Phillip standing at the window, staring out across the boundless sea. The missing person case remained open, the search for Johanna long since called off.

The sight of the sun setting across the horizon grew more breathtaking with each day. At night, the water danced lightly across the sand, and you could hear the wind singing. If you listen even more closely, you could also hear the faint sound of voices traveling inside the wind.

"Lord Commodus."

"Johanna."

15

COACH

There were only three seconds left in the fourth quarter, with only one point separating the score between the Bears and the Hawks. It had been a banner football season for the Hawks under head Coach Bryden's direction. A harsh, no-nonsense taskmaster, Coach Bryden accepted no excuses when it came to football. His philosophy, "The game must be played, the game must be won at any cost."

He was aware of the locker room jokes bantered about behind his back, and he could care less about the hatred fermenting throughout the squad. Coach Bryden only cared about winning, no matter who got hurt in the process.

The coach had just called his last time-out. It was fourth down with twenty-three yards to go on the thirty yard-line. With a score of 20 to the Bears 21, Coach Bryden knew their only hope was a field goal. He shouted at kicker John Marcuse; jersey number 8.

"It's your ass if you lose this game for me, boy! It'll be your death sentence!"

The official blew his whistle, the team ran into field goal formation, and the coach's words bellowed loudly in Marcuse's head.

John Marcuse was a tall, bull-necked young man who was very gentle and humble. Drafted straight out of college, it was his first year with the Hawks, and for John, it was a dream come true. Pro-football and with a winning team. The Hawks were the season's top pick, and they were close to realizing their third championship.

Marcuse heard the rumors about Coach Bryden while he was still playing college football. The coach was heartless, cold-blooded. But this was Marcuse's big chance at football fame. He was considered the hottest rookie kicker in the league, and besides, he was an optimist, determined not to let anything get in the way of realizing his dream.

Marcuse looked ahead at the goalpost. His breathing became quick and labored. He felt a rush of excitement mixed with a bit of fear. He knew he must not fail himself or the team, and he must not fail Coach Bryden.

"Please, Lord, I have to make this kick!"

"Ready! Set! Hut! Steve Robertson, the quarterback to the

center, called out. The ball snapped to Steve, who quickly positioned it on the ground for the kick.

Marcuse took two giant steps and forced all his strength into his kick. His eyes followed the ball as it moved through the air. The time seemed to have slowed as it streamed in glide toward the direction of the goalpost. Within seconds the official yelled, "It's good!" The crowd roared. The final score, Hawks 23, Bears 21.

That evening, Coach pulled a beer out of the fridge, popped the cap, and swallowed. He let out a loud belch.

The decor was sophisticated and spacious. The living room housed large plants and trimmed furnishings, creating a combined feel of masculinity and elegance. Coach Bryden's career paid him generously.

Coach walked along the dimly lit corridor, passing a trio of stylish vases sitting atop a narrow mahogany table. He entered a bedroom at the end of the passageway. The room was a complete transformation from the contrasting visual images found throughout the rest of the home. A wild array of blue and gold, the team's jerseys' color permeated every part of the room. Football paraphernalia scattered among a host of sports-related objects with one wall entirely covered with the Hawks team members' posters. Hundreds of football cards were plastered and sandwiched between printed banners and pictures.

Muralled on the opposite wall were bleachers filled with cheering crowds. An oversized wooden table positioned beneath a sizable picture window swallowed up much of the room. Opposite the table, placed against the wall, was a small twin bed with three wooden crates stacked at the head of the bed. The two pillows on the bed butted up against the boxes serving as a combination headboard and nightstand, leaving only a narrow space to maneuver between the sleeping area and the outsized table.

The football field's meticulous reproduction covered the tabletop, down to the sidelines, markers, and goalposts. The ground held dozens of miniature toy replicas of what Coach considered to be 'his' boys. Uncanny carbon copies, the exact likeness of every player on the team. The Hawks were everywhere, appearing strangely macabre, as reflections from the room glared back from the windowpane. It was as though Coach Bryden had stepped into an eerie sports museum or nightmare.

Standing just inside the doorway, the long swig of beer spilled from the corners of his mouth. He quickly wiped his mouth on his shirt sleeve, belched again, uglier and louder than before. Taking a few steps over to the table, Coach placed his can of beer on the sideline.

Assembled in huddle formation were Marcuse, Robertson, and every member of the Hawks team. And, there on the sideline with other team members stood a replica of Coach. It was a chilling miniature clone, right down to Coach's overhanging beer belly.

Coach Bryden leaned over the table. His lips began to form words, but no sound muttered from his beery breath. He took a seat on a wooden stool beside the table. He began moving the vivid likeness of himself in a walking motion towards the huddled players.

"You bumbling idiots!" he yelled. "What are you? Men or sissies? You put the team on the line!" he bellowed. "Never let the enemy come that close to your score again! Never!"

His face became devilish and distorted. His eyes rested on the players as he angrily lost himself in play with the motionless figurines.

"What the hell did I tell you? You brain-damaged crybabies!"

Coach screamed at the toy figures, pacing his likeness across the table. Reaching, standing, bobbing up and down from his seated position. Coach continued to move the figurines, accelerating the motion of his image across the table.

"I want winners only! Winners only! Win! Win! Win!"

The practice was off to an early start the following morning. Back in the locker room, some of the players mumbled their displeasure to one another at having to get up so early after their win yesterday.

"Man, I wish he'd get off our backs," said Slogan, jersey number 32.

"I know what you mean," voiced Bones. "I hate the son-of-a-bitch!"

"Yeah... well, the feeling's mutual," Marcuse chuckled, "Coach hates all of us too."

"Okay, girl scouts! Get your rusty asses out on the field!" bellowed Bryden as he entered the locker room. "This ain't no tea party... let's go!"

It was an unusually hot November, and the players were exhausted. The Hawks had already established themselves as the team to beat this year, but Coach was non-stop and relentless. The team needed a rest, but Coach continued to heap drill after drill upon them. They knew they were facing a rough week ahead, and no one looked forward to the next game.

That night, Coach Bryden's voice echoed throughout the corridor leading from his bedroom. "One more time, girl scouts!" he screamed. "It's kill or be killed time! It's not just a game, sissies! It's war!"

At the next game, the fans waved placards and lustily cheered the Hawks on, as they took the lead against their opponents, the Rangers, 17-10. Still, Coach Bryden stood rumbling on the sidelines. He wanted his team to win at all costs, and he wanted them to win big. The coach continued to push and push. To Bryden, the team could never be good enough. He wanted them to be better.

It was the fourth quarter when the crowd went wild.

"Blue 21! Blue 41! Hut! Hut! Hike!" The ball snapped.

Marcuse put everything he could into the kick, and the ball soared. Slogan caught the ball and set sail, running up the left side of the field. He felt the defense's pressure closing in on him and passed the ball to quarterback Steve Robertson who dropped back into the pocket. It was only a moment after Robertson caught the ball that the defense was on him. Robertson fired a pass cross-field to Bones. The crowd became exhilarated.

Bones caught the ball and started to rush the end zone when a 295-pound Ranger rocketed into his back with a driving force that knocked all the wind out of him. Bones' body flew into the air and fell, hitting the ground like a sack filled with sand pebbles. He still held onto the ball as he lay listless below the weight of the Ranger.

Time out was called. Bones' haggard eyes peered up at the cluster of bodies hovering above him. Pain raced from his neck, down his spine, stopping at his waistline. Bones was paralyzed from the waist down. His vertebra fractured during the collision. As paramedics removed Bones from the field, the fans began to boo loudly. Marcuse leads the team in prayer. Coach Bryden showed no signs of compassion, disgusted by the delay of the game.

Not a moment had passed before Coach began to rant, "What are you… jellyfish? The war does not stop just because a man is down! It's called professional football. Not little league! What the hell is wrong with you pantywaist wimps? It's not daycare; it is football. Kill or be killed! Get those rubber legs moving right now! Let's win this game!"

The game ended with a score of Hawks 28, Rangers 16.

It was 2:30 a.m. A dank, musty smell lingered throughout Coach Bryden's apartment. Coach was startled awake from his beer inebriated stupor by what sounded like laughter. It took a moment for his half-awake, tired eyes to focus as he reached to grab the clock atop the nightstand crates for a closer look. He did not see the half-emptied beer can until it was too late.

"Shit!" The coach was too slow to stop it from tipping over on its side. His eyes followed the crawl of the malt liquor down to the floor.

Still feeling the effects of his indulgence, Coach forced his body into a sitting position. He quickly turned towards the direction of the faint sound of movement coming from the table. His eyes became enlarged and fixed as his daunt gaze stared straight ahead. Suddenly, he became fearfully immobilized. A foreboding panic raced through his entire being. The miniature figurines had become animated and started running into field formation.

The head of the Marcuse figurine turned slowly and glared at Coach Bryden. His eyes flared, fiery from intense hatred. The surreal, implausible scene before Bryden could not be real, yet it created a height of dread inside him that rose to panic-stricken levels.

Coach Bryden could not believe his eyes. He wondered if he was still asleep in a dream. In a pathetic whisper, he said, "It's not real... it's not real." Spoken so quietly and barely audible in hopes the figurines would not hear.

The miniature Marcuse doll positioned himself in place for the kick. A strange haze of light fell upon the table, and the crowd of thousands stared with blind intensity from the window's reflection. Coach Bryden turned towards the mural on the wall. It had become alive. The mass of men, women, and children cheered in a furious, unnatural roar. The resounding voices were growing louder and louder.

"Hawks! Hawks! Hawks!"

Bones, bandaged around the waist and spine, seemed to float on legs that barely moved. Bones turned and looked over at Coach; a distorted and monstrous grin nearly covered his entire face. Steve Robertson positioned himself with the ball and yelled, "Blue 42... Blue 41. Hut!" The ball snapped.

Marcuse, smiling wildly, forced what seemed to be the strength of the entire team into the kick. At that moment, an overpowering terror numbed Coach as he stared fearfully at the ball, heading directly at him. The ball seemed to drift slowly towards Bryden. Coach Bryden could not move. Trepidation completely paralyzed his body. As the ball slowly drifted closer to Bryden, he began to quiver and shake. Bryden's mouth became distorted, gaped so wide open, the skin tore at the corners. He tried to scream, but there were only the muddled sounds of fear. As the ball narrowed its distance to Bryden, he could feel his heart exploding from the image before him. It was the head of his prized lookalike, the head of the Bryden figurine.

The crowd roared as they all bounded to their feet.

"Kill the coach! Kill! Kill! Kill!"

The cheers of the boisterous crowd became so overpowering that the petrified gasps of Coach Bryden became lost feeble wails.

Two days passed before Coach Bryden's body was found in his home. A dozen police were on hand, including the medical examiner, who joined the grisly crime scene.

"Jesus!" cried homicide detective Steven Spencer. "What was this guy, some kinda crackpot? Can you believe all this stuff? It's like a sick shrine."

"Best damn coach in the league was what he was, " remarked the police photographer over the faint clicks of his camera's shutter.

"Maybe so, but in my opinion, this goes beyond eccentric. This guy was way past a straitjacket," scoffed Spencer, his eyes racing around the room.

"Look at this, Detective Spencer," one of the uniformed officers called out. "What do you make of this? It looks like somebody just ripped this doll's head off, except I can't find the head anywhere in the room. Do you think the killer took the doll's head with him?"

"Beats the hell out of me," Spencer replied intently. "From this scene, we likely got two nut cases on our hands, and this one lost the bout."

"Maybe the killer was a Rangers fan," mused the medical examiner.

"Maybe the killer collects football cards. I heard some collector cards could be worth thousands of dollars," said the police photographer unemotionally, and still over the faint clicks of his camera.

"Yeah, well, it's impossible to determine what cards might be missing. Time, energy, and effort that we can't spend on this case cause this man's sick!" remarked Detective Spencer, sarcastically.

"Hey, Doc," Spencer's voice now taking on a more serious tone, "What killed this guy... did you find a weapon?"

"No weapon... and I won't know for sure, Spence, not until I get him down to the morgue. But I can tell you this..." the medical examiner continued, "Something beat the hell out of his head."

"Something like what?" asked Detective Spencer, now setting all sarcasm aside. "What type of weapon would it take to pound a man's head like that?" he continued.

"Believe it or not, Spence," the medical examiner hesitated, casting a puzzled look at Spence. "Well, I mean, I don't know for sure, Spence, but... the wounds look like... well they look like tiny footprints. Hundreds of thousands of them."

16

MIDNIGHT

Voices stirred in the man's head as he walked swiftly past an old woman covered in dirty blankets and trash bags beneath the ledge of a doorway. A shopping cart filled with possessions gathered over time shielded her from sight. It was just after midnight when she was startled by his passing, causing her to sink further into the corner like a child playing hide-n-seek in the night. Yet, it wasn't a game, and she knew the dangers to a woman, even an old one alone on the streets at night. The threats were not imaginary. They were real.

The man did not notice the woman as he strode quickly past. The night was dark as the rain fell like splintered pieces of wood against his clothing. There was no movement, no cars, no people in sight. The streets were hauntingly still except for the sound of the pounding rain and his footsteps.

Continuing briskly down the sidewalk, his eyes stinging from the striking rain, fluttered as they raced along the brick row houses lining the streets ahead of him. His bare feet were icy cold and numbing as he paced along the pavement. He was frantic to catch a glimpse of some movement, some life. The voices continued to swirl in his head as his steps took him past dozens of darkened units. His body starting to numb from the cold. Feeling a sense of urgency, his steps quickened.

Desperation grew with each footstep thumping against the wet pavement as he pushed ahead. The wind pressed hard as it whisked past him. Confused, he had no recollection of who he was or how he ended up wandering the streets. His mind began to drift to another place and time.

An endless corridor stretched before him. He was on his back, floating past bare walls and doorways framing faceless images. The voices were loud, whimpering, guttural cries that echoed throughout the passageway. He could not understand the sobbing words but sensed that the utterances were crying out in pain. The sobs frightened him.

Two huge entry doors appeared in front of him.

"Wait," he called out. "Wait! Wait!"

Fearful of entering through the doors that began to open slowly, the man tried to move, but his arms and legs were restrained.

"Wait, what is this? Where am I?" he asked. "Why can't I move?"

His body floated past the doors into a blinding bright light causing him to tighten his eyes shut.

His thoughts abruptly interrupted by the sound of a growling dog started by his sudden approach. The man hastened his stride, passing the dog quickly. He didn't know how many blocks he'd traveled before finding himself standing beside a trash bin alongside the front of a long alleyway. There was no end to the darkness stretching in front of him. The entry to the alley appeared somewhat dry and safeguarded from the wind and rain. Glancing down either side of him at the rows of endless rain-blurred buildings, there was still no sign of movement. He entered the alleyway.

A sickening stench oozed throughout the alley as he fumbled cautiously past the debris scattered along the pathway. He was soaked, cold, and confused. He came upon a dry heap of discarded boxes and clothing. Exhausted, he climbed into the pile of litter, sheltering himself beneath the pieces of clutter. The man lay in the darkness for hours, drifting in and out of a disquieted sleep.

A bright light glowed around the man as he floated through the large double doors. It took a moment for his eyes to adjust to the luminous glow.

Lying on his back, his arms and legs shackled.

"What is this? What am I doing here? Why am I being restrained? Is anyone there?" he cried. "Where am I? Where am I?" He closed his eyes tightly and could hear voices screaming along with him.

When he opened his eyes, he was still in the alleyway, tucked under the cardboard boxes. Ice cold tears streamed down the side of his face. His body shivered in the frigid cold.

As the man pulled the debris closer to his body, he was frightened by a sound across the alley. Glancing over toward the direction of the noise, he glimpsed a large rodent scurrying across the debris. He rested back into the cardboard bedding. As he stared across the alley, his body abruptly stiffened. The sight before him caused an overwhelming sense of terror. Directly ahead, a pair of eyes glared back at him. He slowly took a deep breath to gain control of the palpitations coursing through his upper body. The eyes appeared maniacal, and the man felt faint as blood raced to his head. The eyes remained fixated as they continued to stare back at him.

"Who are you?" The man whispered. There was no reply.

Becoming more frightened by the eyes veiled within the shadowy darkness, he dared not speak again. He sat lifelessly, focused on the haunting eyes ahead of him.

As the night went on, the eyes continued to glare menacingly at him. The man's panic grew fiercer with each passing moment, realizing that the lurid eyes looking back at him had not turned away or blinked.

Light began to bleed slowly into the alleyway. Morning arrived as the chill continued to pierce the air. There was some movement on the street now. A few cars were passing, the footsteps of a passer-by or two. The rain had stopped. The city was awakening, coming to life.

Pushing her garbage-bagged possessions in her shopping cart, the old woman stopped at the covered trash bin at the alley entrance. After struggling to open the lid, she began rummaging through the discarded trash. She glanced at the pictures on the newspaper pages before quickly crumpling the pages tightly and stuffing them inside her tattered clothing for added warmth. There was a half-eaten sandwich, which she quickly snatched up and tucked in a pocket, continuing more rapidly to comb through the debris, searching for more morsels or treasures to add to her cart.

Within the alley, a speck of sunlight fell upon the stiff, lifeless body of the man. He resembled a discarded mannequin, surrounded by the left-over scraps from an unsuccessful yard sale. The stench now rose from his rain-dampened clothing. His ashen face held a wild, dread-driven stare cemented towards the other side of the alleyway.

One could only imagine his fear, so petrified by the alley's frightful visitor, a departed dead, apparition, or phantom of the night.

Standing amid the debris directly across from the man

a large, partially hidden mirror, not more than twelve feet away.

As the old woman continued to stuff newspapers into her clothing, a quick short siren startled her. She glanced at the passing police car. The officer pointed his finger at her and waved her to move along. She quickly gathered her shopping cart and continued down the street as the police car traveled past her.

A woman's voice burst over the car's radio scanner.

"10-96. Be on the lookout for George Joseph Carter. White male, 48 years old, approximately 6 feet tall. Wearing a stolen black overcoat over a blue patient hospital gown. Last seen in the Lincoln Heights District near Mission Road. An escapee from the State Institute of the Mentally Insane. He is schizophrenic with a debilitating fear of mirrors and reflective materials. The hospital said it is severe enough to cause self-inflicted emotional trauma–approach with caution."

"10-4," said the officer.

17

DRIVE-BY

Evan is distracted by the cell phone in his hand and the blare of the radio as he drives down a deserted highway. A stylish man in his mid-20s, wearing an expensive Armani suit, with diamond ring covered fingers, is abruptly startled by the sound of a passing car. Evan turns to see the barrel of a 9 mm handgun pointed directly at him. The cell phone drops to the floor as he attempts to shield himself from the spray of bullets. Several bullets penetrate Evan's body as his car tailspins off the road. His attackers speed off in the distance.

Trapped, Evan lay in agonizing pain, unable to release the seat belt latch. The cell phone now on the floor, inches from his reach, begins to ring. He stares at the caller ID display…Mom. As the phone rings, it triggers a suppressed memory of when he was a child.

Evan is five years old. He runs around the living room, pointing a toy cap gun in all directions. Small puffs of smoke follow the sound of loud pops, filling the room with each pull of the trigger. Evan playfully yells, "Bang-bang-bang!"

His mother calls from the kitchen, "Stop running, Evan. Get somewhere and be still. Sit down and watch the cartoons on TV."

Evan giggles at the cartoon characters, aiming his gun at the coyote on the screen while continuing to utter spirited bang bangs.

The cell phone ring turns Evan's attention back to reality. The caller ID reads Madd-Dogg, Evan's partner and childhood best friend.

Madd-Dogg is kicking a man on the ground who pleads for his life. A sigh of relief is heard from the man after Evan throws him a handkerchief, grateful to have his life spared. Evan smiles, pulls a holstered gun from his jacket. Moments later, the man lay dead as Evan and Madd-Dogg drive away down the alley.

The Armani suit soaked in blood. Evan glances at his limp hand, nearly painted red. The phone rings, the name on the ID... Amanda.

It is a month earlier.

Evan is home, sitting at the kitchen table. Amanda, barely 19, is at the stove, adding two pieces of fried chicken to a dinner plate. She turns to reveal a belly three-weeks away from delivery. When Evan bites into the chicken, he spits it back onto the plate. The chicken is raw in the center. Evan angrily throws the plate at Amanda striking her. Crying, Amanda drops to her knees and scrambles to clean up the mess.

The road is still and quiet. Evan's pain worsens as he grows weaker, his vision begins to blur, and panic starts to set in. The phone rings, and he struggles to see the name of the caller. The text on the ID reads... Dad. A spark enters his blood redden-eyes, and Evan recollects back to being five.

Evan's toy gun is pointed at the cowboy on the TV screen when he hears his father's angry voice coming from the kitchen. Saddened by his mother's tears, he runs and hides at the end of the couch, where he listens to his mother crying.

Later, Evan's father is on his knee, talking to him. His father tells him that he is leaving. He hugs Evan and instructs him to be a big boy, but Evan pleads with his dad, he wants to go with him.

As Evan peers out the living room window, his mother continues to cry in the background. His dad carries a suitcase to his car as Evan pounds against the windowpane.

"Don't go, daddy, please daddy, don't go!"

His father does not look back.

As he drives away, Evan points his cap gun towards his dad's car and whispers, "Bang-bang."

Evan never saw his father again.

Evan's face is dampened with tears as he struggles to breathe. The pain is excruciating; he knows he is dying. Evan begins to pray.

"Dear God, please forgive me."

Evan cringes as he gasps for air, struggling to speak.

"Why did you leave me, dad? Why didn't you come back to get me?"

He pleads for God's mercy and forgiveness for the pain and horror inflicted on others, the reign of terror that led him to this moment.

As his body numbs, he continues to ask for God's mercy and compassion. His words muddled as he continues to pray.

Trapped in the car, it feels as though hours have passed. It has only been minutes when the phone rings again. Evan's vision now blurring from the blood flowing from the wound on his forehead. He struggles to focus on the caller ID text. In his pain, there is a moment of hopefulness as he sees the word… Dad on the ID.

"Dad. Dad, I missed you. I missed you so much," speaking towards the phone as it continues ringing.

"Dad… Dad. I've missed you, Dad. I really missed you. I needed you. I still need you."

As he stares at the phone, his eyes widen as fear consumes his body. He begins to convulse as he gasps for air, frightened by what he is seeing. The text ID does not say

Dad ... it says 'Devil.'

Evan gurgles as blood spills from his mouth. The text slowly changes as Evan draws his last breath. The caller ID display now reads... 'Welcome to hell.'

MY STORY

JACALYN EYVONNE

I will never forget the time after reading a story I had written to a friend, the strange look on his face. It was one of those looks you see in a scary movie when a person realizes they are afraid of you.

I was raised in a home with a mom that loved reading books by some of the most well-known mystery and horror story writers. She worked the graveyard shift at a major county hospital in Los Angeles. When she arrived home in the mornings, her bedtime began, and while she slept, I read her books. Always making sure I left her bookmark in the right place. Reading her books became intoxicating. I loved that feeling of being afraid, finding myself jumping and squealing aloud. It was exhilarating entertainment.

More importantly, I knew it was just entertainment.
Separating reality from make-believe has never been an
issue for me.

I became fascinated with the likes of King, Lovecraft, Stoker,
Hitchcock, Blatty, and Koontz. I began writing my own
stories at a young age and fell in love with the mystery
horror genres. Murder became my velleity, and so did scary
movies.

A graduate of the Academy of Art University in Motion
Picture and Television, I became an independent filmmaker
dabbling in creating some of my own short horror stories. I
both write, direct, and produce. While some of my stories
are splattered in the macabre, many are not.

In my writings, I attempt to develop relatable characters and
offer a plot twist or surprise ending. I have a lot more of
what some might consider crazy thoughts in my head.
However, believe me when I say, "I'm not crazy. I just have
a hungering sweet tooth for eerie."

Wide eyes locked, scouring the darkness
as floorboards creak beyond
the bedroom door
and garbled wails fill the air.
Fear festers as the sounds
grow closer, louder.
Midnight; the moon looks south
veiling itself in tears
wary of the horror that awaits
no sweet dreams tonight
just weeping,
not knowing if there will be a tomorrow.

To contact the Author

Author.JacalynEyvonne@gmail.com

www.StrangeThingsHappenAtMidnight.com